DRINKS AND SINKHOLES

Related titles by S. Usher Evans

PRINCESS VIGILANTE

THE SEOD CROÍ CHRONICLES

THE MADION WAR TRILOGY

DRINKS AND SINKHOLES

Weary Dragon Inn

BOOK ONE

S. Usher Evans

Sun's Golden Ray
Publishing

Pensacola, FL

Version Date: 7/29/23

© 2023 S. Usher Evans

ISBN: 978-1945438578

Map created by Luke Beaber of Stardust Book Services
Line Editing by Danielle Fine, By Definition Editing

Sun's Golden Ray Publishing
Pensacola, FL
www.sgr-pub.com

For ordering information, please visit
www.sgr-pub.com/orders

To RHS4

You and this book

grew in my heart

November 2022

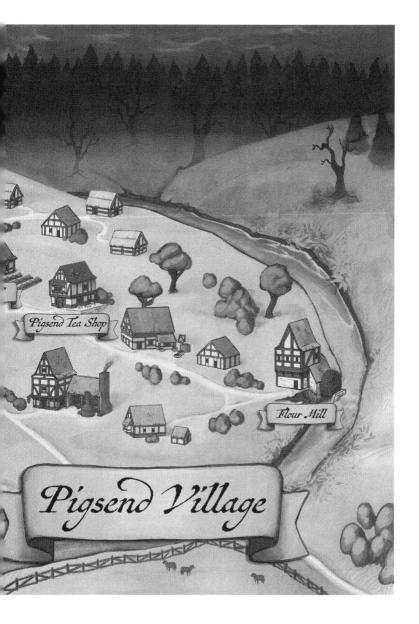

CHAPTER ONE

"*That* is a sinkhole."

Bev stared down into the black abyss, her words echoing in the cavernous space. She'd been on her way back from the twice-weekly farmers' market with a wagon full of produce to serve guests at her beloved Weary Dragon Inn when she'd heard a loud rumbling. Then the ground began to shake, rustling the trees and making the pebbles dance along the road. Bev's old mule Sin (short for Sinister; she'd had quite a reputation once) had brayed unhappily, backing up a few steps before Bev hopped off the carriage to soothe her. Once the shaking stopped, Bev had continued down the road to investigate when the road itself had…disappeared.

"That's definitely a sinkhole, Bev."

Grant Klose had been behind Bev in his own carriage, returning to his farm after selling all his produce at the market. When Bev had come to an abrupt stop, he'd jumped off his carriage to see what the problem was.

"What'dya reckon?" he asked, peering down next to her.

"No idea." Bev rubbed the back of her neck where her short, dark hair reached her shirt. "Couldn't have picked a worse spot, though."

"Could've been in the middle of Pigsend."

"Could've been," Bev admitted with a nod. "But this is a well-traveled road, y'know? Someone not paying attention would go head-first."

Grant nodded. "We should put up a barrier, yeah? I got an axe in the barn. Let's cut down a tree."

It took some time, but between the two of them, Bev and Grant cut down a young sapling near the hole so it fell right in front of it, serving as a very obvious deterrent to anyone coming down the road.

"That'll at least slow them down," Grant said, dusting off his hands. "Do you want to pop over for a glass of lemonade?"

"Wish I could," Bev said, walking to where Sin was eating nearby grass. "Got some new guests coming into town today. Queen's soldiers."

"You don't say." Grant whistled. "Suppose that Queen Meanie likes to get her claws into every inch of her kingdom. Wouldn't be surprised if they were coming to harass the locals before moving on."

"Queen Meanie." Bev chuckled. "That's a good one."

Queen Meandra had come into power some years ago through a violent and bloody war against the previous king. From what Bev had heard, it was quite a spectacle, with thousands of soldiers marching against each other, wizards casting magic, and perhaps even a dragon or two. But the stories had come from the old wine merchants who came back and forth, and they liked to exaggerate, so who actually knew the truth?

Not Bev, that was for sure.

"I'll let the mayor and sheriff know about this." Bev nodded. "We'll see about getting some folks out here to fill this in. Have a good day, Grant."

"And to you, Bev."

The rest of the ride was uneventful, and Bev almost forgot about the sinkhole, except for the new blisters on her hand from swinging the axe. The road into Pigsend wound over hills and by lush fields, still green from the late summer growing season, though there'd been a bit of a drought, so things were on the dry side. In a few weeks, everything would be brown as the weather turned colder, and before Bev knew it, the world would be covered in a soft blanket of snow. But for today, the sun was warm even if the breeze was cool.

"Hey, Bev!" Bathilda Wormwood was barely visible from behind her fence. She only came up to Bev's stomach, with white hair, rosy cheeks, and a smile that could brighten any day. With a huff, she hopped over the fence and waddled over so Bev slowed her mule.

"What can I do for you, Bathilda?" Bev asked.

"When are you going to be baking that magnificent rosemary bread again?" the old woman asked.

Bev blew air between her lips. "I don't know. Wasn't planning on it until the weather turned a bit colder. Best for stews, you know."

"I'd kill for that recipe." She leaned on the wheel with a smile that could've softened even the hardest heart. "Why don't you give it to me?"

"Sorry, dear," Bev said, patting the old woman on the head. "Not for sale. Even for homicide."

The woman huffed and marched away, and Bev just smiled. Nearly every time Bev ventured to the farmers' market, Bathilda asked about the rosemary bread. The legendary bread had been baked at the Weary Dragon Inn for years, the recipe passed down from innkeeper to innkeeper. When Bev had inherited the inn from Wim McKee, the secret recipe had come with it. And Bev wasn't about to break decades of tradition.

She kept on, glancing behind her to where Bathilda was tending her rutabagas and shaking her head. There was something a bit off about her, though Bev wasn't sure exactly what. But it wasn't her business to question people's private lives, so she left it at that.

It wasn't long until Pigsend village came into view. Thatched roofs and stone chimneys reached toward the blue sky, separated by a dirt road lined with sprouts of green grass and plants with white flowers. Perhaps a hundred or so folks lived in the town limits, working all manner of trades that helped sustain the economy. Bev knew pretty much all of them—and the farmers who lived in the fields just beyond—she could say she got along with mostly everyone.

She waved to Bernard Rickshaw as he stood outside the apothecary, feeding his infamous chickens as they clucked about. They weren't as bad as Rosie Kelooke's, who escaped regularly and attacked whoever dared cross their path, but they were numerous and loud. Bernard was good at his trade, but there were always a few feathers in the draughts when ordering from him.

Allen Mackey, the local baker, was skulking down the street, his hands stuffed into his pockets. His thin shoulders were hunched over his tall frame, the curtain of black hair hiding most of his face. He wasn't yet twenty-five and had inherited the bakery from his dear mother two years ago. He hadn't quite gotten her talent with yeast and sugar, or perhaps the young man just didn't care about the legacy of delicacies his mother had left behind. Bev hoped he would get serious about baking one day. But for now, he seemed content to squander the money away.

He glowered at her as she rode by, but Bev just smiled and waved.

"Got any rolls baked today?" she asked. "I got waylaid out on the road and won't have time to bake before dinner. I'll pay you a gold coin for them."

He softened at the promise of money. "When do you want them?"

"Whenever you can deliver them," Bev said. "I'll pay you an extra silver for your trouble, too."

His eyes lit up even more. "Well, absolutely, then. What's the hurry? Got special visitors at the inn tonight?"

"Queen's soldiers," Bev said. "Going to make them a nice roasted chicken and some root vegetables. Market was plentiful today."

He nodded. "I'll have them packed up and sent over within the hour."

"Much obliged."

He walked inside, and Bev just chuckled at the ease with which he was placated. Even as prickly as he was, Bev still carried a soft spot for the baker. His late mother had welcomed Bev into the fold without a fuss, even ensured Bev got a job within a day of showing up here.

And that job had turned into owning the best inn this side of the Stellan river.

The beautiful sight of a green roof, white plaster walls, and the dark wooden accents of the Weary Dragon Inn never ceased to amaze Bev. She navigated Sin around to the back then unhooked the mule and led her to her stall, making sure she had hay and water.

The mule let out a loud bray of approval, almost sounding as if Bev had worked her *too* hard.

"I'm so sorry, Your Majesty," Bev said, patting the donkey on her brown hide. "But we had to stop and get that sinkhole safe before anyone fell in. You know me. Gotta save the world."

Sin just ducked her head into her food trough and kept eating.

"Very well."

Bev lugged all the items inside and found the six whole chickens she'd ordered earlier in the day hanging above her hearth, delivered by either Ida or Vellora, the local butchers across the street. Bev hummed to herself as she prepared the chickens first, creating a mix of butter, crushed garlic, and thyme from her small garden out back. There was *something* about the dirt that made the herbs she grew taste better. She didn't have room or time to tend to a full vegetable garden, so she'd planted rosemary (of course), thyme, oregano, and other herbs to always have something extra on hand for her nightly dinners.

Humming to herself, she chopped the carrots, onions, and fennel from the farmers' market and arranged the pieces around each of the six chickens in separate roasting pans. Then they went into the large, stone oven, and within minutes, the whole kitchen smelled of deliciousness.

"Bev? You here?" Allen had arrived with the rolls. "So uh…that'll be two golds, yeah?"

"Price went up?" Bev smiled as she walked over to her pouch on the counter. If it were anyone else, she would've argued. "Here you go. As promised."

The look on Allen's face said he thought he should've asked for more, but he took his money and left. Bev stood at the door, watching him while wiping her hands on her apron. She shook her head and muttered about young men and their headstrong nature before turning back to clean up the kitchen.

The queen's soldiers were due to arrive in another hour or two—and the chickens were happy cooking, so Bev cleaned herself up, put away her apron, and set out to speak with someone about the sinkhole. Across the street, Vellora Witzel was sweeping up the blood in the butchery and waved to Bev.

"Did you find the chickens?" Vellora asked with a bright smile. She was perhaps the tallest person in town, with thick muscles and long blonde hair that she kept braided down her back. She would've been an imposing figure, except that she was just so darn nice.

"I did. Thank you so much," Bev said. "You haven't seen Rustin around, have you?"

Vellora frowned and shook her head. "No, can't say I have. Is everything all right?"

"Sinkhole appeared on the road outside of town," Bev said. "Once I get these soldiers settled, I'd like to see about getting a group of folks to head out and try to fill it in before someone gets hurt."

"I'm sure the missus will help," Vellora said, nodding toward the front door. "She's inside finishing up."

"Who's asking?" Ida said, walking out wearing a bloodied apron. She barely came up to her wife's armpit, with tawny skin and tight, black corkscrew curls that bounced as she went about her day. She was as slight as her wife was bulky, yet she could hoist a whole cow by herself. Her deep brown eyes lit up when she noticed Bev. "Oh! Hi, Bev. Did you find the chickens?"

"I did," Bev said. She briefly told Ida about the sinkhole, and the other butcher nodded.

"I'd be happy to help," she said, wiping her hands on her apron. "Just let me know when and where."

"Great," Bev said, thumbing toward the city. "I'm headed into town to let the powers-that-be know. If I could ask you two to keep an eye on the chickens for me. Should be cooking for another hour, but in case I'm not back."

"Of course." Ida nodded. "Good luck."

"You're gonna need it," Vellora muttered.

With a soft whistle, Bev made her way into the town square of Pigsend. The town hall building was on one side with the schoolhouse, and the faint sounds of schoolchildren reciting their daily lessons, directly across from it. In the center of the square was a large marble dragon spurting water into the air.

Bev continued to the town hall, pushing open the thick wooden door. Inside was the town meeting space, where the townsfolk would gather to discuss…usually nothing important. The mayor was sitting in her office, her door mostly closed. But on the opposite side was the small office that housed the only law enforcement officer assigned to their quaint little town.

Rustin was broad-shouldered, tanned with curly brown hair and piercing brown eyes—not that Bev could see them. He was fast asleep, his feet kicked up on the desk as he leaned back in his chair. A shiny pin sat on his tunic, which was new. Most everyone knew who Rustin was, so he rarely saw the need to wear his official pin carrying the seal of the queen. But perhaps with the arrival of her soldiers, he wanted to dress up.

"Um…" Bev pushed his foot. "Rustin."

"Hmmm." The sheriff grunted and scratched his stomach. "Five more minutes, Ma."

"Not your ma," Bev said, poking him in the stomach. "Wake up."

He jolted, shock flooding his face as he looked up, then recognition dawned. "Oh, it's you, Bev. You scared me."

"Sleeping on the job?" she asked with a smirk.

"Just trying to get ready for the soldiers," he said. "They aren't…here yet, are they?"

"Not yet," Bev said. "But we've got bigger problems. There's a sinkhole in the road outside town."

"Oh." He blinked, the wheels turning slowly in his head. Brilliant, he was not. "What's the problem?"

"It's in the road, Rustin," she said patiently. "Someone's liable to fall in. We need to fill it before that happens. Can you help me round up some people? Maybe in the morning we can—"

"Sorry, Bev. Would love to help. But I gotta keep myself available to the soldiers." Rustin wiped his mouth as he stood. He gave Vellora a run for her money in terms of height, but Bev thought the butcher might edge him out. "Have you heard why they're coming?"

"You're the one who told me about them," Bev said with a shrug. "I've gotten nothing more than that."

"Yeah, me neither." He rubbed his smooth chin nervously. "Hope they aren't here to replace me. You never know with these soldiers from the capital."

"I mean," Bev cleared her throat, "if you're worried about them thinking you're not suitable for the job, maybe gathering an entire town to help fill a hole would change their mind?"

"You think?" He scratched the back of his head. "I guess that would make me look pretty smart, eh?"

"A real hero," Bev said, nodding solemnly. "Especially if they can't get their wagons around it.

Sin and I sure had trouble. It's *in the center of the road*, you know."

"I see, I see. I'll—"

There was a knock at the door, and a raven-haired, pale-skinned beauty with red lips swept inside with a smile on her face—Mayor Jo Hendry. Her cheekbones were as sharp as her political acumen, and her eyes were as quick as an eagle's. She practically purred as she said, "My dear Sheriff Rustin."

"Ma'am." Rustin all but bowed to her. "What can I do for you?"

"Have the queen's soldiers…? Oh. Bev." Mayor Hendry's dark eyes swept over Bev as if she were disrupting a spell she'd cast on the sheriff. "What are you doing here? Trouble at the old inn?"

"Not at my inn, no," Bev said. "But there's a sinkhole outside of town that needs filling."

"Oh my. Well, that certainly sounds like a problem that is someone else's to solve," she said with a breathy chuckle. "Rustin, I need you."

"Of course!" He practically stumbled over himself as he scrambled after her. "Whatever you need."

"There's a painting in my office that needs to be hung before—"

Before what, Bev didn't know, because at that very moment, the ground began trembling again.

CHAPTER TWO

The trio scrambled to hold onto something sturdy, but it was in short supply as the ground violently shifted back and forth. Paintings and maps slipped down Rustin's wall, and his ink and quill set tipped over, spilling black onto the wooden floor. A vase toppled off a table, and a piece of the ceiling fell just beyond in the town hall room.

It lasted a full two minutes—per the clock on the wall—before things settled.

"What in the...?" Hendry said, her raven hair askew across her face. "What was that?"

"Earthquake," Bev said. "One happened just before the sinkhole appeared outside of town."

"That's ridiculous," Hendry said. "We don't *have* earthquakes or sinkholes in Pigsend."

"We do now," Bev said.

The sound of concerned voices echoed in the town hall, and Bev, Rustin, and Mayor Hendry rushed outside. Bev's breath caught in her throat as she stared at the gaping hole where the dragon fountain used to be. She walked forward slowly, peering down into the second sinkhole in as many hours. This one wasn't as deep, but the beautiful dragon fountain was in pieces on the ground.

"Oh, no," Bev said, putting her hand to her forehead.

A crowd had already begun to gather in the square. The town of Pigsend wasn't all that big to begin with, and everyone lived where they worked, practically.

"What a shame," Bardoff Boyd, the local schoolteacher, said. The schoolhouse was right next to the town hall, so he and his gaggle of students had rushed out when the shaking started. "Has anyone told—"

"My statue! My beautiful statue!"

Ramone Comely, the local sculptor, came running into the square, their hands pressed onto their cheeks. The artist used to work in the big city for some royal benefactor but had retired to Pigsend some years ago. They were always a bit unsettled by changes in the weather and wind, and Bev could only imagine how long they'd be in a tizzy over their statue's destruction.

They stood on the edge of the hole and sighed. "What the earth gives, it takes away." They picked up a handful of dirt and threw it into the pile. "It was garbage anyway. I can do better."

"It was a beautiful statue, Ramone," Bev said. "It's all right to mourn—"

"Ugh, why look in the past when the future is so bright?" They turned and stalked away, muttering to themselves.

Within a week or two, they'd undoubtedly have an even more ornate statue sitting in the town square.

Earl Dollman, the local carpenter, jumped into the hole and walked around, testing the integrity. "It seems it's done growing. May have just happened because of the earthquake. A fluke."

"It's not a fluke," Ida said. She and Vellora had come from the butcher shop. "Bev said she came across one in the middle of the road leading into town earlier today."

A couple pairs of eyes swept to Bev, and she nodded. "That was bigger, I think. I can see the bottom of this one."

"Two sinkholes in one day?" Shasta Brewer, who worked at the tea shop in town, frowned.

Stella, her twin who worked with Barnard at the apothecary, nodded. "Sounds like it's a problem."

"No problem at all," Mayor Hendry said, parting the crowd with ease. "My dear friends, these things unfortunately happen. We live on shifting earth, and occasionally, our fountains get the bad luck of the draw."

"I've lived here seventy years and never seen a sinkhole," cried Etheldra Daws, the semi-retired owner of the tea shop.

"Things happen sometimes," Hendry said. "Either way, we shouldn't concern ourselves with it. It's not as if they're going to show up all over town and swallow our houses."

But the image seemed to unnerve the crowd, who murmured amongst themselves, some rubbing their hands together. Hendry, noticing her error, held up her hands once more and the murmuring stopped.

"Dear friends," she said with a soft smile. "I promise you, there's nothing to worry about. But if it would help you sleep easier at night, I'll put my best people on investigating the cause of these sinkholes."

There was only one person she had at her disposal, and he was staring off into space.

"Rustin," she prompted. "You'll look into it, won't you?"

"Who, me?" He jumped. "Right, yeah. What am I looking into?"

Hendry smoothed the wrinkles on her shirt. "The sinkholes, dear. The one right in front of us and the one outside town. You're going to look into them."

"Right." He turned to peer into the hole.

Bev coughed to hide a chuckle as Hendry took Rustin by the shirt and pulled him close to her to whisper angrily in his face.

Finally, he nodded slowly. "Right. I will investigate the cause of the sinkholes in the town and stop them from happening again!"

"There you go, big boy," Bev said with an affirmative nod.

"And in the meantime," Hendry tossed one long raven lock over her shoulder, "we will need to gather some people to help." She turned to look squarely at Bev. "Since you're so eager to be involved, Bev, why don't you lead the effort?"

She sighed. "I've got chickens in the ov—"

"Glad to hear it!" Hendry cast a look behind her. "Come Rustin, must have that painting on the wall before the queen's soldiers arrive."

Rustin and Hendry disappeared back into the main town offices, leaving Bev to stand outside with her hands hanging by her side and the whole crowd looking to her for guidance.

"I'll keep an eye on the oven," Vellora said with a shake of her head.

"And I'll help you find people," Ida said. "How that woman keeps getting reelected, I haven't a clue."

It didn't take that long to wrestle up a group to help. Ida, of course, would be able to pull a wagon full of dirt all by herself. Earl, the carpenter and Jane Medlam, the mason, offered to help as well.

"What about my oven?" Rosie Kelooke asked. The retired seamstress glared at her two workers, who'd been building a stone oven for her for the past few days. "You said you'd be done already."

"Oh, come now, Rosie," Bev said. "Surely, you can spare them for a few hours."

She gave Bev an apprising glare. "Perhaps in exchange for that rosemary bread recipe."

"How about a piece next time I make a loaf?" Bev said. And based on how many folks had asked that same question, it looked like she'd be baking in the near future.

The old woman agreed to relinquish her help for the afternoon, so Earl and Jane emptied Jane's wagon and headed out of town to get some piles of dirt, with Ida following behind.

Not a few minutes after they left, Vellora returned with a smile on her face. "Those chickens look scrumptious," she said. "Don't know how you do it, Bev, but you never make a bad meal."

"If we're lucky, the queen's soldiers won't show up today, and I can share it with everyone," she said with a grin.

Sometime later, Earl and Jane arrived with the dirt, and Bardoff allowed all his pupils to join in the effort to shovel it into the hole. "It's a counting exercise, boys and girls," he said. "One, two…"

"Three, four…" they chanted, perhaps secretly pleased to be out from behind their desks and in the fresh air playing in the dirt.

Even before the schoolchildren had finished their work, another wagon of dirt appeared, this one courtesy of Ida.

And within three hours, the giant sinkhole in the middle of town was a flat pile of dirt.

"Job well done, everyone!" Hendry said, reappearing in the front door of the town meeting hall. "It's amazing how this town comes together in a crisis."

Beside Bev, Ida and Vellora shared a look but said nothing as they dusted themselves off.

"Haven't seen those queen's soldiers yet," Bev said, glancing at the sky. "Should be here soon, you know?"

"I'm sure they'll be here at a time that's inconvenient for everyone but them," Vellora said with a glower. "You know, considering they think everything belongs to them."

Ida put her hand on Vellora's arm. "Honey, you promised you'd be nice."

"I am being nice. They're lucky they don't get a repeat of the Battle of Press Mountain."

Bev clicked her tongue. "I didn't realize you were a soldier, Vellora. Queen- or Kingside?"

She shifted uncomfortably. "Losin' side, unfortunately. But I don't like to advertise that. They say all's well that ends well, but too many of my fellow soldiers went missing if they announced their loyalties too loudly."

Bev nodded. "I won't tell a soul. And hey, you're free to skip out on dinner if you don't want to break bread with the enemy." She paused, giving Vellora a soft nudge. "Should I be worried those chickens aren't cooked all the way?"

"No, unfortunately, my love of a cooked bird outweighs my hatred for the queen's army," she said.

"And that's saying something," Ida replied with a hearty laugh.

"Well, I suppose I'd better get back to tidying up before they arrive," Bev said. "I—"

A loud trumpet echoed in the distance, drawing the attention of everyone in the square. Five white horses wearing breastplates of gold and green came prancing around the corner, their heads held high almost as if it was beneath them to be in this place. Atop them were five soldiers wearing matching tunics, none of which had a hair out of place or a speck of dirt on them.

"Ahem." The one in front, a sour-looking woman with high nostrils and dark hair pulled into a severe bun at the nape of her neck, looked around the crowd. "Is this..." She lifted her lip in a sneer. "Pig's Butt?"

"Pigsend, you little—" Vellora began, but her wife stopped her.

"Hush, honey," Ida said.

"Yes." Bev stepped forward. "This is Pigsend. You must be the soldiers we've been expecting. I'm Bev, the owner of the Weary Dragon Inn."

The lead soldier's gaze narrowed. "Indeed." She looked around the rest of the crowd. "Why are you all so...filthy? Is this normal for the folk here?"

Vellora snarled. "I'll show you filthy..."

"I think it's best you get her out of here," Bev muttered to Ida.

Ida nodded and gently pried her wife from the crowd. Vellora kept gazing back at them, fury clear on her face, but eventually, they ducked around the corner and were gone.

"We had a sinkhole appear in town," Bev said. "Wanted to fill it in before anyone got hurt. Did you happen to see the one outside of town, too?"

The lead cast a look at her soldiers, three women and one man, who each wore a smirk. "I suppose we assumed that's just how it was out here in the faraway lands. Things just seem so much more *uncivilized*."

"We prefer to call it quaint," Bev said, putting her hands in her pockets and a smile on her face. Wim had taught her to treat strangers with kindness, even if they were keener to spit in her face. "But I'm sure you're tired. I have a nice meal of roasted chicken and vegetables, along with some good ale, waiting for you. Nice beds, too. Some of the best in town."

"It's the *only* inn in town, is it not?" the soldier asked.

"Well, yeah. That's why it's the best." Bev grinned.

Bev led the five soldiers the short distance to the Weary Dragon Inn and did her best to let their judgmental whispering roll off her shoulders. Even the most cantankerous of the travelers usually softened after a hot meal and a warm sleep in their bed.

"If you'll leave the horses in the pen, I'll make sure they're fed and watered this evening," Bev said as she opened the gate. "And then I'll show you to your rooms."

They dismounted, their shiny boots looking strange against the dark brown dirt in the yard. Swinging their capes around themselves, they marched one-by-one into the inn, saying nothing to Bev. The only one who stayed behind was the lead, who'd introduced herself as Karolina Hunter, though she'd said nothing else about herself.

"Innkeeper," she said.

"Oh, my name is Bev."

"Bev?" She sniffed. "That's an…interesting name."

"Well, funny story about that," Bev said with a chuckle as she held her arm out to guide Karolina into the kitchen and beyond. "About five years ago, I stumbled into town without any idea who I was or where I'd come from. Luckily, Pigsend is full of kindhearted folks, and one, Wim McKee, took me in. Said that it didn't take much to know how to be a beverage wench, so that's what I did."

"Ah." She cleared her throat. "So you're… named for a beverage wench?"

"More or less," she said, opening the door to the main dining room. The other soldiers milled about with their arms crossed, muttering to each other as if bored.

"And you have no clue who you were before you arrived in town?"

Bev beamed. "Not even a little bit."

"And that doesn't..." Karolina eyed her suspiciously. "Bother you at all?"

Bev shrugged as she walked behind the counter. "Pretty happy with my life these days. Whatever I was doing before, I suppose it's probably best left in the past." She plucked five keys from their hooks on the wall. "Shall we do one room a piece, or would you like to double up to save some of Her Majesty's gold?"

"One per room is fine," Karolina said, putting a large bag of gold on the counter.

"Then it's five gold pieces per night, which includes your dinners, of course," Bev said, pulling out the old inn-keeping book and writing *Queen's Soldiers* onto five lines, along with the current date. "If the boy across the way is feeling useful, he'll sometimes drop off muffins in the morning, too."

"And tea?" one of the soldiers asked.

"I've got some from the shop in town," Bev said. "Plus, I add a little extra to it. My garden out back has all kinds of herbs ripe for the picking. Just let me know what you fancy, and I'll get it up to your room in no time."

Bev smiled, expecting to see a softening of the jaded expressions, but there was none.

"Just the rooms, please. We do not require dinner," Karolina said, pushing the gold across. "We will pay per night until we've completed our business in town."

"And how long will that take?" Bev asked, a little miffed that they were declining what smelled like an amazing dinner.

She started, giving Bev a scrutinizing look. "As long as it takes to complete. Which is none of your business, innkeeper. So I suggest you keep your large nose to yourself and tend to your duties."

With a huff, Karolina swiped the keys off the counter and distributed them amongst her compatriots. One-by-one, they marched upstairs without a second look. As they disappeared, Bev covered her face with her hand, frowning. She'd thought she had a regular-sized nose.

Then again, compared to the slick-haired, clean-shaven, well-dressed city dwellers, Bev supposed she looked a little rough.

"Guess I'd better tend to the horses," she said to no one in particular, wiping down the counter absentmindedly. "Hopefully, they're better company than their riders."

CHAPTER THREE

Unfortunately, the horses weren't any nicer. Bev didn't know how a group of animals could act so high and mighty, but they sure managed it. They even seemed to look down on the oats and hay Bev had raked into their stalls for them to eat.

"A thousand apologies, dear guests," Bev said with a chuckle. "But hopefully, your soldiers will be done quickly, and you can get on your way."

There were only five stalls in the stable, so Sin had to be relocated to the pen outside. The old mare didn't seem to mind, though Bev did give her a few extra carrots and a warm blanket over her back.

"There you go, old girl," Bev said, patting her on

the rump. "It'll probably be warmer out here. Better company anyway."

Even though the soldiers didn't want dinner, they weren't the only ones who'd come a-calling. Vellora had pulled the chickens from the oven while Bev was messing with the sinkhole, but they were quite warm and the drippings still liquid. Bev put the birds on her carving board and made a quick gravy from the fat and herbs stuck on the bottom of the roasting pans. The scent made her mouth water, and she was secretly glad the soldiers weren't going to partake. More for her.

The root vegetables were brown and caramelized, so she spooned those onto a large serving platter, adding a sprinkling of herbs for an extra kick. Finally, the chickens had rested enough, so she took her time removing the thighs, then the wings, then the breasts in one piece off the bird, then cutting them in half. She arranged the pieces nicely onto another wooden serving platter and added another sprig of rosemary for garnish.

She brought each dish out of the kitchen and into the main room, where Earl had already started a nice fire in the hearth. He and Etheldra were regulars for dinner, and the old woman's eyes lit up when Bev carried in the chicken.

"My! What a feast!" She clapped her hands as she rose and ran over, grabbing a wooden plate.

"Any chance of the rosemary bread today?"

"Not today," Bev said with a sad shake of her head. "Too busy with that sinkhole. But Allen Mackey dropped off some rolls."

Nobody seemed keen to grab one.

"Do we need to save any for those…uh…guests of yours?" Earl asked, already laden up with five pieces of chicken on his plate.

"They declined to eat with us tonight," Bev said. "Eat as much as you want."

Ten minutes later, Bardoff joined them, followed by Apolinary McGraw, the seamstress, and Gore Dewey, the blacksmith. Bev began to worry that she might not have had enough, but the stream of people ended with Max Sterling, the librarian, who helped himself to a single drumstick.

With only a thigh and slice of breast left, Bev made herself a plate with the remaining food and poured herself a pint of ale before joining the group at one of the three circular tables. The conversation was, of course, about the sinkholes, about what could be causing them, and whether Sheriff Rustin was going to be able to handle the investigation.

"Of course he isn't," Gore said. "Couldn't tell his left foot from his right, even as a schoolboy."

"Give him time," Earl said.

"You know," Bardoff said. "I think I heard one of my kids say they saw a new gnome mine pop up on the south side of town. Maybe they've gotten a little too close to the city. Hit something."

"It's possible," Bev said with a nod.

"Unlikely." Etheldra scoffed. "Dwarfs know more about the ground than anyone. That they'd be so careless *and* risk the ire of the queen? It's a ridiculous notion." She leaned forward on the table. "Now those soldiers who showed up in town today…"

"Don't be silly, they showed up after the sinkholes started happening," Apolinary replied. "And even if they hadn't, what would they have to do with anything? They ain't got magic or special skills or any of that. Just boring old queen asskissers."

"Keep your voice down," Max hissed. "You don't know what they're in town for. Could be rooting out traitors."

Apolinary scoffed but stuck a rutabaga piece with her fork and stuffed it in her mouth instead of answering.

"Bev, what'd they say to you?" Earl asked.

"Not much," Bev said, putting down her fork and knife. "Just that they were in town to complete some business, and when it was completed, they'd leave." She opted to leave out the comments about her large nose. "I don't think they mean any harm."

"They're probably just salty that they got

assigned to come out to the sticks," Gore said. "Maybe one of 'em ticked off the queen, you know? Got the short end of the stick?"

"Possibly," Bev said. "They certainly didn't look pleased to be out here."

"What got ol' Vellora so mad?" Apolinary asked. "She looked ready to take one of their heads off."

Bev wasn't going to say, but Gore saved her the trouble anyway. "She was in the army. Kingside. Suffered some great losses. Miracle she escaped alive. Even more of a miracle she hasn't been thrown in jail. Queen says all's forgiven, but..."

Everyone at the table grew somber as the rest of his words went unsaid. Sometimes, Bev was grateful she had no memory of the war. She often wondered if perhaps she'd been a participant, and what had transpired had been so horrific she'd decided to black out her memory instead of living with the trauma.

That or she'd just fallen off her horse wrong.

"Well, I'm sure they'll be done with their business just as soon as they can and things will return to normal," Bev said. "At least, normal enough for anything that happens in Pigsend."

⁓

"No need to clean our rooms, keeper," Karolina said the next morning.

The soldiers yet again looked immaculate—this

time wearing what appeared to be regular tunics fashioned like their armor and brown boots instead of the shiny black ones. The other four said nothing as they filed out the front door, and Karolina brought up the rear, closing the door with a flourish.

"Good morning to you, too," Bev said with a shake of her head.

But she didn't have time to dwell—chores needed doing. Bev stuck to the routine she'd learned under Wim's careful tutelage. First, hauling her bucket out to the well to get water. Then she washed the rest of last night's dishes, scrubbing the roasting pans and serving platters until they were pristine and ready for another day of making delicious food. Then, she set to the rest of the kitchen, dusting the shelves and checking on her stores of flour, sugar, lard, as well as her vegetables.

"Flour needs a refill." She might bake her infamous rosemary bread for her taciturn guests, and if that was the case, she'd need to visit the miller later today. She checked her root cellar, though more out of habit. Yesterday's visit to the farmers' market had set her up for at least two or three days.

With the kitchen clean, Bev turned to the rest of the common areas, dusting, sweeping, wiping. Today, she washed the windows and beat the rugs, too, just to spruce up the place for the guests.

She walked out to the pen where Sin was grazing

on the hay Bev had set out earlier and patted her on the nose. "Feel like going on an adventure today, Sin?"

The old mare shook her head.

"Well, tough," Bev said, leaning on the fence. "We need to take a trip to the miller so I can make some bread."

"Oh, is it time to make your infamous bread already?"

Mayor Hendry came sliding into the open area behind the kitchen, her lips a brutal red and her eyes smeared with dark shadow. She wore an unusually bright smile as she peered into the open kitchen door.

"Are our guests still sleeping?" she asked.

"No, sadly. The lot got up and went to work about an hour or two ago," Bev replied. "But I'll be sure to let them know you were asking about them." She walked to the stable, retrieving Sin's harness. "Any luck on the cause of those sinkholes yet?"

"Oh, no. But you know it's Rustin's top priority," Hendry replied, running a slender nail along the edge of her lips. "Do you happen to know where the soldiers went?"

"I don't," she said. "They were pretty clear that they didn't want to share their business. And to be honest, I don't need to know it."

"I see. Well." She brightened. "I'll be sure to

come by later to snag a piece of that delectable bread and perhaps have a chat with them."

Bev didn't have the heart to tell her the soldiers hadn't wanted to eat the night before—and she had a feeling the same would be true tonight. "About that sinkhole," Bev said. "We need to get the one outside town filled. I'm not sure I can spare the time today, so if you could—"

"Toodle-oo, Bev, dear!"

Bev sighed. First, the miller. Then, perhaps after, she'd spare some time to fill another sinkhole.

The miller was on the east end of town, situated on the banks of Pigsend Creek, and Bev always enjoyed the ride. It was another beautiful, late summer day, with puffy white clouds against a crystal blue sky. The sun was warm and the breeze pleasant. Bev could really spend all day out here, enjoying the fresh air. But if she wanted to get the bread rising in time, *and* work on that sinkhole, she couldn't waste any time.

Sonny Gray was a cheery man who still managed to lift ten-pound bags of flour with ease, even considering his advanced age. Bev paid two gold coins for two sacks, plenty to get her through the next few weeks.

"Beautiful day," Sonny said, putting his hand on the flour sack. "Just can't ask for anything better."

"Did you happen to feel that earthquake yesterday?" Bev asked.

He shook his head. "Didn't know about it. Where was it?"

"There were two," Bev said. "One on the west side of town, and one that swallowed the Pigsend fountain."

"Goodness me!" He put his hand to his chest. "That's a shame. Any idea what's causing them?"

"None," Bev said. "Just the strangest thing, you know?"

"I'll tell you what's strange. The Pigsend Creek!" He nodded toward the barely-spinning mill and beckoned Bev to follow him. "Barely a trickle these days."

"We haven't had much rain," Bev said with a frown as she peered down into the gully. The water line on the rock was at least a foot higher than the current one, and it was barely touching the mill wheel. "That's pretty low. You might have to get out and push it."

It was intended as a joke, but Sonny wasn't smiling. "Can't be milling any flour if I don't have water in the creek."

Bev nodded, wiping the smile from her face. "I'll be sure to say a prayer for rain. We all need it."

That seemed to cheer the miller up. "Say, I do have a favor to ask, since you're here. I have an order for Mackey's kid that he hasn't picked up yet. D'ya think you could bring it to him? He hasn't paid for it yet, but—"

"How much?" Bev asked. Surely, the baker would pay her back for her trouble, especially after overcharging her for the untouched rolls the night before.

"Five gold coins."

Bev reached into her purse and paid Sonny. "Here. I'll get him to pay me back next time I see him. Go on and load 'er up."

Sin brayed in protest.

"Oh hush. We can do nice things for people," she said, patting the mule on the butt.

It was quite a large order, and Sin had trouble getting started, but once they were moving, the mule seemed fine with it. Bev let herself look at the trees and search for any signs of changing colors—none yet, but it wouldn't be long. She waved hello to Freddie Silver and his new husband Hans, who were out tending to their pigs. They'd been married perhaps six months and were still known to wander into town, staring dewy-eyed at each other.

Today, though, they were both in coveralls as they fed the pigs.

"Afternoon, Bev!" Freddie called. "Got quite a wagon full today, don't you?"

"Helping young Allen out," she said with a

shrug. "What are you gonna do, eh?"

But the old mule was huffing and puffing, so Bev decided to stop where Pigsend Creek came close to the road, near Trent Scrawl's farm. She unhooked the mule from the wagon and led her down the banks to the trickle of water.

"Sorry it's not much," Bev said, glancing at the sky. "I suppose these pretty days do come at a cost, eh?"

She let Sin rest for a bit, but the responsibilities waiting back at the inn beckoned. Bev still needed to get the bread on, visit the butchers, dice up the root vegetables, pull some more rosemary to dry… the list went on and on.

"Well, girl, let's get going," Bev said, rising to her feet.

The mule seemed in better spirits, and Bev even helped her get the cart going by pushing it then hopping on.

The walk back into Pigsend was slow, but eventually the town came into view. The young apprentice Gilda Clamber was outside the blacksmith's shop, her face covered in soot as she waved at Bev. "Afternoon, Bev!"

"After—" All of a sudden, Sin stopped walking, tossing her head agitatedly.

"C'mon, girl, almost home," Bev said, reaching forward to pat her on the hindquarters. "Promise that—"

The ground shook violently again. In the nearby blacksmith shop, three scythes toppled, barely missing Gilda as she dove for cover. At Etheldra's house next door, the nice flower vases fell off their table and shattered onto the front porch.

Sin began to buck and bray, so Bev jumped off the wagon to grab her by the harness and keep her steady. But it was hard to keep herself upright as the ground moved beneath her. Finally, after an eternity, it stopped, though Bev's hands shook as she petted Sin's nose.

"It's all good, sweet girl," Bev said, more for herself than the mule.

She looked around. That was a big one—bigger than the one in town. She expected to see a sinkhole nearby, but there didn't seem to be anything except agitated wildlife tumbling out of their burrows. Bev exhaled a little. Perhaps just a lot of shaking and no sinking.

"Whew." She patted the donkey's nose. "We should—"

"Bev! Bev!" Ida came running around the corner. "Come quick, it's the inn!"

Bev's heart stopped as she scrambled to her feet and ran through the town faster than she would've thought possible. As she passed the town square and caught a glimpse of the perfect thatched roof, she let out a sigh of relief. But it didn't last long.

There was another, gaping sinkhole steps from the front door. Bev's newly cleaned welcome mat had been sucked in, and the front shutters were askew, but the inn itself looked intact. But only just.

"Well, this is…" Bev put her hand to her head, letting out a breath that was equal parts relief and panic as she peered into the hole. "This is something."

Chapter Four

"Yeah, you got lucky, Bev. Guess ol' Wim is keeping an eye on his place after all."

Earl came over right away to assess the damage. Bev held her breath as the old carpenter walked the perimeter of the inn, running his hands along the plaster walls and inspecting them closely. To the old carpenter's estimation, had the earthquake shaken just a few seconds longer, Bev's entire livelihood would've met the same fate as the dragon fountain.

"What should I do?" Bev asked. "Fill in the hole?"

"Might not be that easy, Bev," he said. "The ground's unstable. We can fill it with rocks and dirt, but there's no telling if another earthquake wouldn't just undo it. Don't know if you've been to the fountain yet—"

Bev shook her head.

"But all the work we did yesterday... There's already another sinkhole forming there." He shook his head. "The thing to do is to figure out what's happening and why—and put a stop to it."

Bev wiped her hands on her apron. "Supposedly, Rustin's on it."

"You really trust that nincompoop?" Earl asked, climbing out of the hole with his rickety ladder. "Look, between you and me, I think there's something funny going on. You don't go from no earthquakes and sinkholes to three in as many days."

"What kind of funny?" Bev asked.

He shrugged. "Haven't the foggiest. But—" Earl quieted immediately, his gaze going behind Bev.

The five soldiers had appeared, with at least one looking aghast as he peered into the hole. The others just looked annoyed at the inconvenience.

Karolina cleared her throat as she stepped forward. "Is everything all right here?"

"Yes, just dealing with some...unexpected sinkholes," Bev said.

"I can see that." She paused. "Is the inn structurally sound?"

"As sound as ever," Earl said with a bright smile.

Bev appreciated the white lie from the carpenter. As much as she didn't like the soldiers, she needed their gold—especially considering Allen owed her five coins for picking up his flour.

Karolina turned to Earl, casting her snooty gaze on him as if he were a pile of donkey dung. "And who are *you* to make that assertion?"

"Uh, I'm Earl. Carpenter." He pulled his cap off his head. "Ma'am."

"Well, Earl the Carpenter, should we wake up in the bottom of this hole, I will be sure to lodge an official complaint," Karolina said with a sneer. "If the inn is structurally sound, we will be purchasing another night. I suppose we can—"

"Go through the kitchen door," Bev said, nodding toward the back. "Feel free to leave the gold on the counter, and I'll get everything taken care of." She glanced at her pocket watch. "It's a bit early for dinner, but I'll be getting things going in a minute. If you—"

"Don't trouble yourself. We don't need dinner."

And as before, they marched in a single-file line around the corner of the inn and disappeared.

Bev let out a long breath, shaking her head.

"Jeez, and I thought Etheldra was mean," Earl said with a whistle. "How long are they staying?"

"Not a clue. They pay by the night and said they'll leave when their business is concluded."

"Great." Earl chuckled. "Guess it's nice to have a mostly full inn, though, eh?"

"Especially if I've got to worry about repairs," Bev said, nodding to the hole. "I need to talk with Hendry about this. She's got to make this a priority before someone really loses their home. Maybe she'll see reason this time."

Earl chuckled. "Don't count on it." He paused, wiping his hands. "What's…uh…on the menu tonight, Bev?"

"Oh, um. Probably vegetable stew," Bev said with a wince. Now that she had a sinkhole to worry about, there wasn't a chance to get on baking the bread—let alone roasting any meat tonight. "Maybe Allen can help me out with a loaf or two and make it heartier."

"Well, you've certainly got enough flour," Ida called, leading Sin and Bev's wagon of flour down the road. The butcher had pulled three bags from the cart to lighten the load on the mule and carried them on her shoulder as if they weighed nothing.

"Oh my goodness!" Bev put her hand to her head as she rushed to meet the butcher. "So sorry, Sin. I completely forgot about you with all the chaos. Thank you, Ida. You're a lifesaver."

"It's all right. That's what friends are for," Ida said. "But seriously, what do you need with all this flour?"

"Half of it's Mackey's," Bev said, taking the reins from her and patting Sin on the muzzle apologetically. "Sonny Gray asked me to deliver it since he's been hanging onto it for days."

"Are you sure Allen paid for it?" Ida asked, casting a wary look around. "I hear he's been skipping out on payments to folks in town."

Bev didn't want to tell Ida *she'd* paid for it, knowing she'd get a lecture about being too nice. "I'm sure that's not my business," Bev said with a shrug. "But if you'll be a dear and let him know it's here, I'd be appreciative. After I get all this unloaded, I'm going to find Hendry and have a good talk with her about this sinkhole."

"What do you think she'll say? Just pass you off to Rustin again?"

Bev didn't doubt it. "If she does, I might have to pull the Big Option."

Ida gasped and covered her mouth. "Oh, Bev, you naughty girl. You wouldn't."

"I would and I will," Bev said with a firm nod. "But I don't want to. They can get…unwieldy."

"For all our sakes, I hope the mayor listens to you," Ida said with a grin. "All right, I think that's the last of yours. Let me go tell young Mackey he's got a delivery. And make sure he minds his manners."

The soldiers might not have wanted to eat dinner, but Earl and the others would be waiting in the dining room. Before taking off for the mayor's office, she washed and prepped the vegetables, making sure everything was ready to drop in once she returned. This stew recipe was one Wim had given her on the rare occasion she found herself short on time. "Emergency Vegetable Stew" he called it, swearing that the combination of carrots, onions, and celery plus barley, mushrooms, and some dark leafy greens to round it out would fill any belly that needed it.

Then again, she glanced at the ceiling where the soldiers were presumably sleeping, there were bellies that seemed impervious to the smells emanating from the kitchen.

With the vegetables chopped and ready, Bev decided she was at a good stopping point and pulled off her apron. She passed by the mirror near the front door, checking her face for dirt smudges and making sure her short hair was at least managed before hanging her apron by the back door and walking out. She made the trip around the inn, inspecting every inch she could see of her beloved building to make sure it was still in one piece. But as she came toward the front, and that damned sinkhole, she spotted movement across the street at the bakery.

Allen was skulking out his own back door, wearing a long, black cloak that looked like he was about to travel somewhere far away and high boots that had seen cleaner days.

"Hey Allen," Bev called. "Wait up!"

If he heard her, he didn't show it, as he took off toward the north, headed toward the dark forest beyond town. It was best avoided by the townsfolk, as it had been known to house unsavory characters of the magical and human variety from time to time.

Bev took off behind him, telling herself she was walking to the mayor's office, but she couldn't help following the path Allen had taken, just to make sure. Perhaps he was going somewhere else. She didn't want to assume the worst, especially about her neighbor.

Yet he kept walking beyond the last houses and down the overgrown road toward the dark forest. Bev stood on the edge of town and put her hands on her hips, sighing. Then she stepped out beyond the village and raised her voice.

"Hey Allen!" she called, putting her hands to her mouth to get his attention.

The young baker went stick straight, like he'd been caught doing something wrong. He slowly turned around, his face pale as Bev walked up to him.

"What do you want?" he asked. "Why are you following me?"

"Because you didn't say anything when I called out to you five minutes ago," Bev said, putting on the most generous smile she could muster. "Where are you going?"

"What does it matter to you?" he snapped, his shoulders hunching around his ears. "Are you stalking me?"

"Just wanted to let you know that I picked up your flour order," she said. "It's sitting on my cart, if you want to grab it. I'm headed to the mayor's office right now or—"

"Why'd you have to pick it up? Now I owe him money for it." Allen scowled and kicked the dirty ground, muttering to himself.

Bev's brows rose. "Well, because Gray asked me to, and I paid for—"

"Just keep your big nose out of my business," he snapped, turning and skulking into the forest.

Within minutes, Bev lost him in the brush. She reached up to hold her nose, checking the shape again. Nope, still the usual size. Why everyone seemed to be obsessed with her nose lately, she hadn't a clue.

But she couldn't help watching the space he'd left. Allen had always been a bit cagey, but lately, it seemed to have gotten worse. Bev had chalked it up to losing his mom to the plague a few years ago, but...no. This was more recent than that. Something was amiss with the young baker, and she owed it to his late mother to keep an eye on him—even if he was snippy with her.

"It'll be there for ya when you come around," she said, with a sad sigh.

Allen's strange behavior not withstanding, Bev did have to get back to the inn to get dinner ready, so she turned and headed straight to Hendry's office. She stopped as she came into the town square. The flat dirt patch where the fountain had been already had another hole forming.

"It's been sinking all afternoon," Bardoff said, locking the door to the schoolhouse.

"That doesn't bode well for me," Bev said. "Got another one in front of the inn."

He turned to her, his brow furrowing before he shook his head. "We need to figure this out before someone *really* gets hurt."

"Agreed. I'm headed to the mayor now to... well...to see what she's done about it thus far."

He snorted as he swung his cloak around his shoulders. "Good luck to you, Bev."

She'd need more than luck. When she walked inside town hall, Hendry's door was open, and the mayor herself was seated at her desk, a large painting of Queen Meandra behind her. Bev was certain that used to be a painting of the mayor herself, which perhaps explained why she'd wanted Rustin to help her swap it out with the queen's soldiers arriving.

"Ah, Bev," Hendry said, looking up. "Did we have an appointment?"

"No, but this can't wait," Bev said, standing in front of the desk. There weren't any seats, perhaps to discourage people from lingering in her office. "I suppose you heard there was another sinkhole."

"I hadn't."

"You didn't feel the earthquake?"

"I perhaps heard a little rumble but thought it must've been the mason moving her bricks," she said, sitting back. "Where's this one?"

"In front of my inn," Bev said. "And Earl thinks it might get worse if there's another earthquake too close. The sinkhole in the town square is already dropping again."

"My, my." She leaned toward the right. "Rustin, dear."

The sheriff was visible from the other side of the meeting hall. "Yes, ma'am?"

"How is the sinkhole investigation going?"

There was a too-long pause. "Very well. Should have an answer soon!"

"See?" Hendry said with a saccharine smile. "Nothing to worry about."

"Jo," Bev said, wishing there was a seat so she

could get eye level with the mayor. "You can't just sweep this under the rug. Literally, because the sinkholes will swallow the rug."

"It's just not a good time for this," Hendry said with a thin smile. "We have the queen's people in town. I'd hate for her to lose confidence in the way this town is run and send someone else."

"I can certainly appreciate that," Bev said. "But surely she wouldn't fault you for something outside your control." Bev paused. "This is…outside your control, right?"

"Don't be silly. Of course it's outside my control." She straightened the papers on her desk. "But you know the queen. She likes things orderly. No waves, no attention. Better to just let these soldiers do what they need to do and move on to the next town. Then we'll conduct a full investigation."

"I can't wait until they move on," Bev said. "Every passing minute is another chance for the sinkhole in front of my inn to get bigger. If I lose the Weary Dragon…" She didn't even want to think about it. "We have to do something. Now."

"I'll convene another group to fill in the hole," Hendry said.

"No, we have to figure out what's causing them," Bev said with a heavy sigh. "You know I hate to do this, Jo. But you leave me no choice."

Hendry's eyes widened. "Bev, don't—"

"I officially ask for a town meeting on the matter of the sinkholes."

The mayor let out a sigh of exhaustion. "You can't be serious."

"I am," she said. "And you know the rules, once I officially ask—"

"Which is why I *am asking you* to please reconsider your official ask. We haven't had a town meeting since…"

Since someone had been poaching the chickens out of the town's front yards. Five hours of back and forth where everyone in town got to have their say about what they thought the problem was and how it should be solved only to have Shasta Brewer's old bloodhound find a den of foxes who'd set up shop in the forest right outside town.

"We need answers, Hendry," Bev said. "And I'm sorry, but we needed them yesterday. I think once we convene the meeting and get a plan in place, you'll see that it's the best course of action. *And* the soldiers will be able to report back to the queen that you're a proactive mayor doing whatever it takes to protect your town."

She sighed, rubbing the bridge of her nose. "Very well. I suppose I will make the announcement. Tonight. We'll have a town meeting on the matter of the sinkholes."

CHAPTER FIVE

There weren't very many laws in Pigsend, at least
ones that needed enforcing. The usual ones applied:
be kind to one another, keep your property and pets
to yourself, and don't make a racket after midnight.
But the most important rule, one not even Hendry
could say no to: if a citizen asked for a town
meeting, there *would* be a town meeting—that
evening.

Word spread as quickly as gossip, as every person
in the city limits was invited to attend. Even some of
the farmers who lived just outside joined the ruckus.
The small room between the sheriff and mayor's
office would be filled with people all the way to the

back, each clamoring for a turn at the podium to say their piece. It very often resulted in some tangents, and it was all Hendry could do to keep everyone on track. But usually, there was *one* person in town with some solid good ideas, and Bev was banking on that someone to help solve the problem of the sinkholes.

The town meeting would begin at sundown, so Bev prepared her vegetable stew and put it out in the main room, along with clean bowls and spoons. With Allen skulking around wherever he'd gone, she wouldn't have any bread or rolls to go with it, so she hoped the barley would be enough.

But as it turned out, she'd done all that work for herself alone, because not even Earl and Etheldra showed up to partake. So Bev ate as much as she could stomach, left her dishes in the sink, and exited through the back door.

As she rounded the corner to the front, she examined the sinkhole for a minute, examining it to see if it had gotten any worse. Perhaps a few more pebbles had fallen from the upper level into the hole, but the inn looked all right.

"Goodness, what a mess," Ida said, coming to stand next to her and placing a comforting hand on her arm. "Hopefully, we'll collectively come up with some answers."

"I hope so, too," Bev said, covering her hand and squeezing. "Thanks again for bringing Sin back earlier."

"She was a bit salty to have been left," Ida said with a chuckle as Vellora locked up the butcher shop across the street. "But she'll be all right."

"What's your bet for how long this will last tonight?" Vellora asked with a smirk as she approached. "I say two in the morning."

"Oh, don't be silly. We'll be there until at least four," Ida replied with a giggle as she wrapped her arm around her wife's. "Especially if Eldred Nest gets going with his wild conspiracy theories."

"Oh, leave the old man alone," Bev said with a smile. "You know I didn't want to do it, but Hendry didn't seem to understand the gravity of the situation. At least now I can get her to focus on it."

They strolled through the empty streets, as most folks had already made their way toward the town hall where the meeting was to take place. It was peaceful with only the sound of evening birds chirping in the distance. The sky was a beautiful purple-pink as the sun disappeared for another night.

"Are you going to put forth any theories, Bev?" Ida asked.

"Someone mentioned there a new gnome mine," Bev said. "Seems like a long shot, but best not to leave any stone unturned."

"True," Vellora said. "I still think it's those

smarmy soldiers. Waltzing in here like they own the place and being secretive."

Bev didn't argue. "I'm sure you're not the only one with that theory. But we'll see what the crowd comes up with once we get inside."

There was a buzzing in the room even before Bev entered. It seemed every person in town was concerned about the sinkholes, because they were packed into the room. But that was a good sign. The more minds, the better chance *someone* might have an answer that made sense.

"Bev! Ida!" Earl was waving them down. "Saved you three a spot."

They made their way over, bunching up next to the old carpenter in a space not meant for three people. But it was the most room they'd get, considering there was a full house.

Not two minutes after Bev had sat down, Hendry and Rustin emerged from the mayor's office, making their way toward a small table in the front of the room. This was the usual setup—the mayor and sheriff at the front of a long center aisle that bifurcated the room. Speakers would stand before the table, facing the mayor as they said their piece, and those waiting would be queued up behind them.

Hendry didn't look pleased to be conducting a meeting, but she rose and plastered on a smile. "My dear friends."

Almost immediately, the entire room went silent.

"As is tradition here in Pigsend, if someone asks for a town meeting to discuss a matter of importance to the community at large, we must oblige their request. And so you have all been invited here today to discuss the matter of the sinkholes that have appeared in town."

"Hear, hear!" cried Jane Medlam.

"I know you're all concerned," Hendry continued. "But before I open th e floor to concerns, I'd like Sheriff Rustin to give his preliminary report on his discoveries."

Rustin rose from his chair with a piece of paper in front of him. He loudly cleared his throat. "There are three sinkholes in town. The first occurred to the east of town along the main road. The second occurred in the middle of town. And the third right in front of the Weary Dragon Inn. They are all different in size, shape, and depth." He folded the paper and sat back down as the crowd murmured angrily.

"Great job, Sheriff Useless," Ida muttered.

"What?" He huffed with a frown on his face. "It's been a day. And the queen's soldiers have had me running around all over the place."

Hendry seemed unsurprised by his lack of

findings. "Now that we have that out of the way, I open the floor to the citizenry to offer solutions, theories, and anything else that might be on your mind."

"Ugh, we will be here all night," Vellora muttered. "She must really not want us to stay on track."

"Maybe she actually knows what's going on and doesn't want to tell us," Ida replied.

"You're turning into Eldred," Bev said, nudging her. "Let's see what the citizens have to say before we jump to conclusions."

~

"And another thing, Trent Scrawl's produce looks far too healthy for the amount of rain we've had."

Bev tilted her head back, releasing a sigh. As predicted, the town meeting had very quickly dissolved into a free-for-all on the grievances of the town. Herman Monday, a farmer who lived on the west side of town, had been at the podium for at least twenty minutes, ranting about everything from the state of his produce to his crosstown nemesis.

"Mr. Monday," Hendry said, leaning on the heel of her hand. "There is no such thing as too-healthy produce."

"He's just trying to smear my name before the Harvest Festival," Trent cried, standing up in the back of the hall. "And that garden of his won't grow because he never waters it!"

"You shut your mouth, you ornery old fool!"

"Please, gentlemen," Hendry said, holding up her hands. "Do either of you have anything to add on the subject of the town meeting?"

"Er, no." Herman cleared his throat. "But I bet you that no-good scoundrel Trent Scrawl has something to do with it!"

"You watch your back tonight, Monday!"

"Thank you both," Hendry said.

Despite his clear desire to stay on the podium, Herman walked back to his seat, casting a wary look around him at his adversary.

"They've been fighting like that since they were boys," Ida whispered to Bev. "My mom told me once that Trent stole Herman's girlfriend and they never got along again."

That was news to Bev. She eyed the butcher. "You've been in town your whole life, right, Ida?"

She nodded. "My family's been here since... gosh, since it was founded, practically. Never been farther than Sheepsberg." She glanced at her wife. "Just got lucky that Vellora decided to wander through here when she did."

"I'm the lucky one," Vellora said, reaching across to squeeze her wife's hand.

"All right, all right," Bev said, as she was

crammed between them. "Save your lovey-dovey for your own house."

"I'm telling you, I've seen mole people around town!" Eldred Nest, a farmer who lived south of town, was ranting at the front of the room now. "They're behind this confounded shaking. They have a whole city underground, you know!"

"You've got to be kidding me," Ida muttered. "Not this again…"

"Yes, Mr. Nest," Hendry said with a sigh. "You believe mole people live under the town."

"I've seen 'em!" he said.

"Where would we find these mole people?"

"We just gotta start diggin'," he said, mimicking the act. "Diggin' and diggin' and diggin' until we reach their little holes and *then*—"

"Thank you, Mr. Nest," Hendry said. "We'll certainly put that as an option to explore. Who's next?"

Next up to the podium was Dane Sterling, another farmer who lived along the road to Gray's mill. He nervously took his hat off, as if he weren't used to speaking in front of a crowd. His words came out as more of a whisper.

"You'll have to speak up, Mr. Sterling," Hendry said. "If you'd like to be heard."

He shifted. "I's just saying," he began, this time louder. "About three weeks ago, I saw a horde of small creatures coming down the road. They had the queen's signet on them, you know. Royal gnomes, I think."

Hendry sat up in her seat, but didn't seem surprised by this. "Yes?"

"They set up shop maybe half a mile from the edge of my farm. Big explosions at first, dust covered all my cows." He twisted his hands around his cap. "Anyway, might be worth lookin' into."

"That is certainly an option." She turned to Rustin. "Please make note of that."

Rustin rose and walked to the chalkboard borrowed from the school and wrote *Gnomes*. But he hadn't even finished before several voices rose in protest.

"Hang on, those are *royal* gnomes," said Rosie Kelooke, coming to stand. "By law, we can't stop them from doing their work. They're protected by the queen. Their work is *very* important."

"They're busy digging up gems for a new crown," Vellora muttered. "Very important, my butt."

She wasn't the only one who felt that way, as Vicky Hamblin stood up and declared almost the very same thing. "This is our town. It was ours before the queen laid claim to it. And she can't just go around sending her minions wherever—"

"Minions?" Rosie gasped, putting her hand to

her heart. "Our queen doesn't have *minions*. She has servants who are doing important work on behalf of the crown."

"Wow, I didn't take Rosie to be such a loyalist," Bev said with a frown.

"Oh yes," Ida replied, casting a wary look at her wife, who was growing a bit red in the face. "Darling, keep your tongue. You don't need to draw attention to yourself. Others will argue your point."

Vellora nodded but clenched her fists so hard her knuckles were white.

Vicky Hamblin was already making her way through the crowd to argue directly with Rosie. She was perhaps twenty, in apprenticeship with Apolinary, who'd taken over when Rosie had retired. Vicky usually had lots of opinions at town meetings. In fact, there was one a year ago about possibly creating a new offshoot of Pigsend Creek to flow closer to the farmlands and she spent over three hours describing the environmental effects of the change. Needless to say, the proposal was declined, mostly because people wanted her to stop talking about it.

"I'm sure the gnomes aren't the only possible reason for the sinkholes," Hendry said. "But it was proposed, so we will investigate." As Rosie let out a gasp of protest, Hendry added, "With all the respect the queen's chosen servants deserve, of course."

That didn't seem to placate her too much, but she sat down with a scowl on her face. Vicky, too, found her seat again, but she was poised and ready to come back for another round if needed.

"Who else has a theory on the sinkholes?" Hendry asked, wearily.

The town meeting continued well into the night, and despite Hendry's best attempts to keep things on track, the only item on the chalkboard seemed to be the gnomes.

"Maybe we're about done with this," Bev muttered to Ida, whose eyes were drooping.

"Hope so," she whispered back with a yawn. "I'm ready for bed—"

"Bev," Hendry called, her laser eyes focused on Bev in the crowd. "You haven't spoken yet. You're the one who called this meeting. Perhaps you have something to add?"

Bev nudged Vellora, who'd fallen asleep on her shoulder, so she could extract herself from under the butcher's heavy head. Once freed, Bev slowly made her way to the front podium.

Hendry seemed eager. "Well? Do you have a theory to add?"

"No, I don't, but I think the gnomes are our best bet," Bev said, rubbing the back of her neck. "I do, however, worry that Rustin might not be the best person to...uh...follow up on this investigation."

The sheriff himself was snoozing, his mouth open and a drop of drool falling down his cheek.

Hendry glanced at him with a bit of a helpless expression before turning to Bev. "And why is that?"

Bev hesitated. She couldn't outright insult Rustin's intelligence. "Well, technically, he works for the queen, doesn't he?" Bev said, nodding toward the small pin on his chest. "Might be a bit of a conflict of interest in case they *are* the ones responsible."

"I agree!" Vicky said, standing up.

"Then who do you recommend take on the task of speaking with the gnomes?" Hendry asked, leaning on her hands. "Because if your quarrel with Rustin is that he works for the queen, you'll have that same issue with me as well." She gestured out into the crowd. "Who in Pigsend is the *right* person to investigate?"

"I don't know, but—"

"Perhaps you, then?" Hendry said. "Since you're so *motivated* to do this right."

Bev held up her hands. "I can't. I've got a quintet of soldiers in town—"

"Oh, the soldiers can take care of themselves," Hendry said, rising. "And I'd be happy to ensure they have all they need at the inn. Might give me a chance to talk with them, since they've been keen to avoid me up until now."

She clapped, sending a wave of waking through the crowd, most of whom had fallen asleep.

"Good news, citizens of Pigsend. It seems we've come to a passable conclusion on the matter at hand." She smiled. "Bev will pay a visit to the gnomes outside town to ask if they have had anything to do with the sinkholes. After all, who can say no to our beloved local innkeeper?"

Bev expected to hear arguments, but instead, she heard murmuring in approval.

"Oh, come on," Bev said. "I don't have time—"

"All in favor?"

"*Aye!*"

"All opposed?"

Bev spun around, gazing at the crowd and praying someone—anyone—would say something. But not even Rosie Kelooke, the queen's local cheerleader, said anything. In fact, she looked *pleased* with this outcome.

"Then it's settled." Hendry banged her gavel. "Bev, we look forward to hearing your report as soon as you find out what's going on."

Chapter Six

"Serves me right for opening my big mouth."

Bev, Ida, and Vellora walked back together in the quiet night. The town meeting had dispersed quickly, with most of the townsfolk eager to get back to their beds after a long night of arguing. But Bev had taken her time, and her two friends had stuck around as a show of support. There wasn't another soul on the street, nor were there candles lit in any of the houses. It was quite lonely, and Bev was grateful for the butchers—especially as the sun would be up in a few hours, and she still had her chores for the day along with this new, large task.

"You know, it's probably for the best," Vellora

said. "You had a point—Rustin's not the right person for the job."

"And I am?" She sighed. "I know nothing about gnomes. Or where to find them. Or how to talk with them about anything."

"Oh, they're just people, like us," Ida said with a wave of her hand. "Just tiny. And magical. I think."

"One of the few who are still allowed to be," Vellora said with a dark look.

"You know," Ida said, tapping her finger to her chin. "I bet you could find something useful at the Pigsend Library."

"Like what?" Bev said.

Ida shrugged. "Maybe a book about gnomes? Something that might give you an idea of why they're in town before you go traipsing up to their front door. I always like to know who I'm dealing with."

Beside them, Vellora had grown quiet, her lips pressed into a thin line as they walked the dark streets back to their houses.

"Vellora?" Bev prompted. "You okay?"

"Do you know much about gnomes, honey?" Ida asked.

"No." She sniffed, a disgusted look on her face. "Just that they're little sniveling creatures who serve the queen. One of the few magical creatures who got put on a pedestal instead of…"

"What do you mean?" Bev asked.

She shook her head. "Look, all I know is that *certain* creatures are allowed to be who they are—and those creatures usually have some skill the queen wants. Whatever the gnomes are doing, I'm sure it's not to the benefit of Pigsend." She crossed her arms. "I wouldn't be surprised if they *were* responsible for all this. It would be just like the queen to send her minions to the outskirts of her kingdom and cause loads of damage."

"Let's let Bev talk to them before we jump to conclusions," Ida said softly, putting her hand on her wife's arm. "Look, we're home. I think we'll all feel better after a good night's sleep."

"I'll *feel* better when the stench of that queen is gone from this town."

And with that, Vellora stomped across the threshold of the butcher shop and slammed the door behind her.

"I'm sorry about her," Ida said. "She doesn't talk much about what happened in the war, and I've never pressed. But anything having to do with the queen has always made her…"

"No apology necessary," Bev said with a smile. "And I won't judge her if she skips out on coming across the street until the soldiers are gone."

"You're a saint, Beverage Wench," Ida said with a small wink. "You know, I really think we need to come up with a better name for you."

Bev chuckled. "I've gotten so used to it now, I'd hate to be called anything else."

~

As predicted, sunup came way too early, and Bev's desire to stay in bed was in direct conflict with Wim's voice in her head, reminding her that a clean inn was a prosperous inn. Not that there was a boatload of travelers coming through these days, and the soldiers seemed to already think Pigsend was dirty. But habit and dedication roused her from her comfy bed and nest of quilts and sent her to the washbasin.

Dressed and ready for another day, Bev set to the usual tasks—sweeping, dishes, wiping down her workspace in the kitchen, tending to the horses and mule out back. She kept a watchful eye on the clock, moving quickly so she could get to the library the moment it opened. Time was of the essence. She didn't want to see if another earthquake would make the sinkhole worse.

When the clock struck five 'til ten, she put aside her washrags and apron and closed the door behind her. Sin was still in the pen, having finished her breakfast, and seemed to be waiting for a carrot.

"Not today, ol' girl," Bev said, patting her nose. "Are you being a kind host to our guests?"

She brayed loudly in protest.

"They'll be gone soon," Bev said. "I hope."

The Pigsend library was a quaint little building with two dark wooden doors on the western side of the town square. Bev had heard from travelers that the library in the capital was bigger than the whole town of Pigsend and filled with nearly every book and tome that had survived the war. Even if it was all Queenside literature, it was something to behold —one could live a thousand years and never read everything within its walls.

The same could, perhaps, be said for the Pigsend library, except the reader would die of boredom. Most of the tomes were almanacs and recordings of harvests, weather events, and other important things that occurred in the town. The sinkholes, for sure, would end up there once the cause was found. The actual selection of books about anything else was quite small, so it was a long shot. But she wasn't about to visit a home without knowing at least a little about the host.

The bell dinged and the clock on the town hall chimed exactly ten as Bev pushed open the heavy door. On a stool behind the counter sat Max the librarian. He perhaps should've retired already, but it was hard to find anyone willing to apprentice with him. His curly white hair was the only thing visible of his head, as it was pressed into his arms, and he was softly snoring. Bev hated to wake him, but she didn't have much of a choice.

She gently shook his arm, earning a snort of surprise as he sat up and blinked heavily.

"Oh, Bev," he said with a yawn. "Late night, eh? What can I do for you?"

"Well, since I've been unilaterally voted to investigate our sinkhole problem," Bev said with a sigh, "I figured I might learn a bit about gnomes. Never met one myself. Don't want to go in uninformed."

"Understandable, understandable," he said, slowly inching off his stool. "Well, I don't have much, but I should have an old encyclopedia of magical creatures. Outdated, of course, because the queen stamped out half the magical population."

"Everything except the things that benefitted her," Bev mused quietly as he disappeared.

"What was that?" Max asked, poking his head out from the stack.

"Just something Vellora said," Bev said. "I don't remember the war, so I don't really know much about what happened in the aftermath."

"Yes, yes, the amnesia. Certainly tricky."

"So you say the queen made sure anything magical was destroyed?" Bev asked.

"That's what they say, but you know how these things go."

Bev tilted her head back to look at the stacks.

"It's just a bit strange to think that one person could be powerful enough to snuff out entire races of creatures."

"Well, perhaps some of them did survive," he said. "Just went underground, you know? Hiding in plain sight." He reappeared with a thick book in his hand. "But this should have the information you need about the gnomes. *They*, at least, are certainly not gone."

"That's quite a book," Bev said. It was three inches thick, dusty, with a worn leather cover.

"Is there anything else I can do for you, Bev?"

"No, but I appreciate the help," Bev said, pulling the book toward her. "With any luck, I'll have this sinkhole problem solved by nightfall."

~

Bev brought her prize back to the inn, setting up on the front counter just in case someone came in looking for a place to stay. Within the first few pages, she was entranced. Every page was filled with drawings, histories, quirks, descriptions, major events about creatures big and small. They were organized alphabetically, but Bev took her time turning the thin pages as she skimmed the information.

Finally, she reached the "G" creatures, slowing her skimming to look at each creature's name until she found them.

GNOMES

It is thought that gnomes descended from the bwbachons, house creatures of the fae, but their exact origin isn't quite known. They are a proud race, easily swayed with fine gifts and compliments to their craftsmanship. Most usually found in large, transient nests that can consume entire valleys as they extract magic from the soil itself. One will know they're near a gnome nest by the prevalence of heliotropes—green plants that contain delicate white flowers—and pink fountain grass.

Once they've completed their excavation, the gnomes will return the land as they found it, leaving only heliotropes and fountain grass as evidence of their stay.

Bev closed the book, sitting up and rubbing her chin. It wasn't much, but at least she now knew what to look for—the book had a very helpful drawing of both plants—and had something of an insight into what made the gnomes tick. She didn't have many gifts to give; not much was worth anything here at the Weary Dragon Inn, save maybe a nice loaf of rosemary bread. But that would take most of the day, and Bev didn't really have all the time in the world to—

"Innkeeper."

Bev jumped, having been too engrossed in the book to notice Karolina and her four compatriots standing behind the front counter.

"Yes, sorry." Bev closed the book but made sure to leave a piece of parchment to hold her place. "What can I do for you?"

"We will be staying another night," she said, casting her gaze down. "What are you reading?"

"Just…" Bev sat back. "Say, you lot are from the Queen's Capital, right? You've probably seen more than a few gnomes in your day."

The soldiers snorted, but Karolina remained stoic. "Why do you say that?"

"Well, I hear they're pretty aligned with the queen," Bev said. "I've been asked to investigate the sinkholes, and I thought I might check with them to see if they're the ones creating disturbances. What do you know about them?"

Karolina pursed her lips. "We're soldiers. We don't hobnob with creatures the queen employs. We simply follow orders."

"I'm sure you do," Bev said with a smile. "Just figured you'd have more of a chance of knowing what they're about than I would."

The other soldiers snickered, and Karolina hissed at them. They cowered and ducked away. She lifted her chin. "If I were you, innkeeper, I would steer clear of the gnomes. They can be quite temperamental creatures and require more than what I'm sure you can provide them in gifts in order to cooperate."

"Unfortunately, I don't have much of a choice," Bev said. "If I don't put a stop to these earthquakes, my inn will be at the bottom of a sinkhole."

"Then search elsewhere," she said. "Because I guarantee you, the gnomes have nothing to do with these earthquakes. And you might find yourself in hot water if you accuse them of such." She slapped another five coins on the table. "Just some friendly advice."

"I thought you said you don't deal with the gnomes?" Bev asked with a curious look.

"Like I said, just some friendly advice."

She nodded to her compatriots, and together, they exited through the kitchen.

Bev thumbed the money they'd given her and slowly slid off the stool. Upstairs, under a loose floorboard, she had a small stash of gold coins that she'd saved over the years. It was supposed to be for emergencies, but if saving the inn didn't count as an emergency, nothing did.

She counted out ten gold pieces, hoping it wouldn't cost that much to speak with the gnomes, and that they were much nicer creatures than Karolina had made them out to be.

Bev dressed in her finest tunic and pants, polished her boots, and ran a comb through her hair, checking her appearance to make sure she didn't have an errant streak of flour on her face. When she was pleased with her reflection, she strapped the small bag of coins to her inner thigh and headed out the door.

"Going out for a bit, Sin," she said, patting the old mule on her nose when she came to seek a treat. "Sorry, don't have any carrots for you. Need to visit the market again."

The mule brayed unhappily.

"Hopefully, today will be a good day," Bev said, glancing up at the sky—looked like rain. "And we'll have answers and we can all go back to normal."

Her wagon was in the same spot as the day before, laden with flour. She sighed. Allen Mackey still hadn't come to get his wares. She would need her cart back eventually, especially if she was going to fill in the hole in the front of the inn. And she could do with the five gold pieces he owed her.

But since it looked like rain, she grabbed a spare blanket from the horse stable and covered the cart before walking to Mackey's bakery. The front door was locked, and the usual assortment of baked goods weren't visible in the window. The oven wasn't on, either. It didn't even look like he was home.

"Allen?" she called, looking up. "Are you there?"

No answer.

"Well, okay. If you are there and ignoring me, your flour is gonna get wet if you don't get it," she said. "I gotta go take care of business, but if you want, I can help you move it—"

"No use in yelling at nothing," Vicky Hamblin said, walking out of the seamstress's shop. "He hasn't been home all day. I've been watching."

Bev quirked a brow. "Oh yeah? Why's that?"

Her face turned red, and Bev had to hide a smile. "Just, you know, worried about him. I like to get a muffin before work. Haven't had one in a few days." She cleared her throat. "No other reason."

"Uh-huh," Bev said. "Well, if he does happen to skulk on back to his house, please let him know that I've covered his flour with a blanket, but he really does need to get it inside before the weather turns."

"I will." Vicky twisted her hands together. "Are you going to see the gnomes?"

Bev nodded. "Hopefully, we'll have a good answer for all these sinkholes before more show up."

Chapter Seven

With a spring in her step and a whistle on her lips, Bev walked down the dirt path toward the northeast. As she left the village behind, she kept her eyes out for heliotrope and pink fountain grass.

She had an inkling where Dane lived, but still stopped to get directions from Trent Scrawl, who was out working in his front fields. "Just over there, Bev."

"Sounds good." She leaned over the fence to admire his wheat, reminded of Herman Monday's accusations at the town meeting. "That's quite a bumper crop you've got so late in the season."

He nodded, a piece of wheat in his mouth. "Just

lucky, I guess."

"Amazing you've still got this much, considering we haven't had much rain," Bev said. The threat of bad weather had cleared and now it was a beautifully sunny day again. "Must have some kind of green thumb."

He beamed. "Well, I can't say I'm any different from anyone else. But I surely will have a stake in this year's Harvest Festival prize! Maybe I'll finally knock off ol' Herman Monday. You know he's gotten the top spot for the past ten years, at least. But that pumpkin over there…" He nodded toward the gourd sitting in the back of the farmer's patch. It was sizable, indeed, bigger than Bev's head. And there was still a month until the festival.

"I'm sure you'll give him a run for his money," she said, pushing herself off the fence. "I'd better get going, though. Nice chatting with you."

"Next time you walk by Monday's house, do me a favor and see how big his pumpkin is, will you? Wanna know what the competition's like."

Bev just laughed as she walked away, waving. The Harvest Festival brought all the farmers into town, and some folks from beyond the small village. The inn was usually packed for dinner, and Bev always made sure the rosemary bread was plentiful.

But, she thought sadly, if she didn't figure out what was going on with these sinkholes, and the inn was demolished, she'd never be able to host a single person again.

As she left the farmer's property behind, the ground got a little…soggy. She frowned and lifted her boots, now covered in thick brown mud. She glanced at the sky. Unless there'd been a *very* local rainstorm, there didn't seem to be a reason for all this water—especially considering the nearby Pigsend Creek had been low.

She turned back toward Trent's house. The path of wet ground led all the way to his place.

"Interesting."

With a wide leap, she sidestepped the muddy road and got back on hard ground.

Farther up the road, Dane was also in his fields, though his crops looked much more puny than Trent's. He waved at her from across the way and put his hands to his mouth as he called to her. "Looking for the gnomes?"

Bev nodded.

"Take a left at the fence end and keep going over the hills. You won't be able to miss them!"

Bev waved her thanks and did as instructed, finding herself off the beaten path and into the rolling hills outside Pigsend. As she climbed, small, white flowers dotted the ground, similar to the drawing in the encyclopedia. But she didn't see pink fountain grass yet, so she kept on.

Dane had said she couldn't miss the gnomes, but as the sun grew higher in the sky, Bev began to wonder if she'd made a wrong turn. There were plenty of heliotrope flowers, but no sign of anything out of the ordinary.

Finally, she spotted the fountain grass wafting in the breeze and more heliotrope farther ahead, almost curling up the hillside in a path. She put on a burst of speed as she crested the hill then her eyebrows rose sharply.

"Oh…my."

The entire landscape had been taken over. All the green grass—gone. It was nothing but rock and dust and small creatures scurrying about. They didn't come higher than Bev's knee, but she hadn't expected them to.

More impressive was the miniature industry they'd built in the valley. The gnomes poured pebbles and rocks into small carts that were carried along on a suspended rope across the worksite until they were dumped into a pile on the other side. Creatures the size of mice carried the larger pieces, and even the gnomes themselves had bags of pebbles on their backs. Everyone was moving with purpose, and none of them noticed the large human standing over them—until one did.

He was an ugly little thing, with an overly wrinkled face and leathery skin that was perhaps just dirty. His ears were nearly the size of his head, and his chin was long and pointed. He began stomping and squeaking, but Bev couldn't understand what he was saying.

"So sorry." She knelt to his level. "Can you repeat that, please?"

"I said," he said, his voice so high it almost hurt her ears, "you are trespassing on the grounds of Her Majesty Queen Meandra. Please leave or we will be forced to make you leave."

Bev didn't want to test that theory. They were small, but there were a lot of them. "I'm here in peace, on behalf of the village of Pigsend." She pointed toward the town. "Right over there. I… uh…" What was the best way to phrase this? "If it's not too much trouble, I'd like to speak with whoever is in charge of this mining operation. We've had some trouble lately, and wanted to make sure that it wasn't…" She considered her words. "Make sure that your great operation here wasn't *unintentionally* impacting the town."

The gnome screwed up his tiny face. "Well, I don't see how or why it would be, but…" He eyed the pouch on her leg. "I suppose I *might* be able to fetch our foreman. Perhaps."

Bev noticed his gaze and pulled out a coin. "It's very much appreciated."

He took it and ran into the hills, and Bev just

hoped she hadn't given him a coin for nothing.

Judging by the sun, at least an hour had passed. Though she'd seen no sign of the foreman or the gnome she'd given the coin to, she'd had a chance to really watch the gnomes work. They seemed indefatigable, walking into the small holes dug in the ground and coming out with more rock. But even after sitting here watching them, she still couldn't understand exactly *what* they were digging for.

"Pardon," Bev asked as one drew close enough for her to speak to. "What are you guys looking for?"

"That's our business," she squeaked.

"Oh, I know, but I was just…curious what the queen is interested in?" Bev handed her a gold coin with a smile.

The gnome took it and stuffed it inside her shirt, though it barely fit. "The queen asks us to look for magic. We excavate the ground, looking for it, and bring it back to her when we find it."

"Magic?" Bev frowned. "There's no magic in these parts. At least not the kind seen in the city."

She chuckled. "You know so little. There's magic everywhere. It runs in veins in the earth. Sometimes it gets bigger, sometimes it gets smaller. But it's always there. Knowing where it runs the best is our job for the queen. And we are very good at it."

"So…are you finding a lot of magic here in Pigsend?" Bev asked, handing her another coin.

"Not a lick of it," she said with a shake of her head. "It's like there's a concentration of magic here that we can't yet find. But rest assured, we won't be deterred. If we don't find it here, we'll pack up and continue to the next town."

"Oi!" The first gnome was back. "You! Human!"

Bev pointed to herself. "Me?"

"The foreman will see you. Make sure you take care to walk in the places I tell you."

⁓

Bev had to twist into some weird positions to cross over the worksite, but she did. And when the small gnome led her to a hole that was his height, she supposed she shouldn't have been so concerned with her clean tunic and boots. Leaning on her elbows and knees, she shimmied inside the hole and down the shaft, following the gnome and thanking her lucky stars she wasn't claustrophobic.

But the close quarters only lasted a few feet before Bev was led into a large cavern. Cool air hit her cheeks as she stood upright fully, gazing at the cave that stretched out before her. Was this always here, or had the gnomes made it?

"Human!" the gnome who was guiding her barked. "Don't dilly-dally."

Bev followed, marveling that they'd built another complex system of pulleys down here pulling rocks out from where they were being actively dug to the surface. There didn't *seem* to be any magic, as the other gnome had said, but Bev's eyes were untrained.

A squat, round-looking gnome with an even more wrinkled face, larger ears, and pointed chin came walking through the mess, his gaze firmly on Bev. She knelt, doing her best to avoid any of the scaffolding around her, and offered a kind smile.

"Good—"

"You say you have come to speak with me on behalf of Pigsend?" the foreman said, interrupting her.

"I have," Bev said with a nod. "I don't know if you've noticed lately, but there've been some… earthquakes happening."

A twitter of laughter echoed from all around her as the gnome scoffed. "We have to shore up this cave every time it happens. Yes, we've *noticed*."

"Well, um…" Bev again tried to come up with a politically neutral way to phrase it. "We were wondering if…*you* had anything to do with them? And if so, if you could…stop?"

The entire cave went silent, and Bev felt a thousand small eyes focused on her.

The foreman took a step forward, absolute

disgust on his face. "How *dare* you insinuate such a thing? Do you think us so careless, human? We are the purveyors of the earth and rock. We take the utmost care in the management of the soil. It is our *job*."

Bev begged to differ, considering the damage they'd wrought on the hillside just beyond this cave. "I mean no offense, I promise. I'm sure if it *was* you, it was unintentional."

"It was *not* us," he said. "We aren't even close to Pigsend."

He beckoned her, and she awkwardly got up to follow. He led her through the cavern, down a cramped tunnel that she could still walk upright in, but barely. He carried with him a torch that lit the way, but it was very hard to see anything.

"Watch your feet!" he snapped.

She'd almost stepped on a gnome who was the color of the rock around them. He raised his fist in anger at her, and she winced in apology. The tunnel grew smaller so she had to crawl on her hands and knees, and then finally…she could go no farther.

"I'm gonna get stuck if I keep following you," she said.

The gnome sighed and kept walking, but he didn't have far to go until he reached a wall. "This here is the end of our mines. It's the closest we'll get to any civilized land, else we'll have to make things much harder for ourselves." He put his hand to the rock. "It is our *calling* to do our work with as little impact to the natural world as possible."

"But…" Bev twisted on her hands, "you've ripped all the grass out of the hill out there?"

He snorted. "And when we leave, you'll never know we were here."

Bev blew air between her lips. "Okay, so if it's *not* you, what in the heck is going on?"

"The rivers are being disrupted," he said, turning to look up at something Bev couldn't see. "The humans who live in your village are doing it."

Bev frowned. "How?"

"That's your job to figure out," he said. "And you'd better do it quick, because it's impacting *our* work, and we don't like to have to rebuild our worksite every time one of you stupid humans takes too much from nature. Now leave before we carry you out."

The sun was beginning to set by the time Bev shimmied out of the gnome hole, and she had a disappointing walk back to the village. As much as she wanted to believe otherwise, her gut told her the gnomes were telling the truth. Everyone from the foreman down had seemed aghast that she'd even *insinuate* carelessness in their work.

The rivers are being disrupted.

Well, there was only one river in Pigsend, and one couldn't really call it that. The large Stellen River came from the city though the countryside, fed by tributaries, including the Pigsend Creek. But the river itself was at least three days' ride from here —too far to really affect anything.

She slowed. The Pigsend Creek *had* been really low lately. But she'd chalked it up to the lack of rain.

But what if it isn't?

It seemed preposterous, really, to even consider that someone in town was *doing something* to the creek. Besides that, the gnome had said *river* not *creek*, and while they were both streams of water, one was decidedly larger than the other, and—

The ground moved beneath her feet. This was— thankfully—a short one, and didn't seem to move much. But Bev's thoughts flew to the inn as she raced toward the village.

Before she even got there, she saw who the unlucky villager had been this time. Rosie Kelooke's brand-new brick oven was now at the bottom of a sinkhole in her backyard.

"Oh…my…" Bev said, joining the crowd already assembled.

Earl and Jane stood over the remnants of their hard work, each wearing a look of annoyance and sadness. Rosie was cursing the sky and the ground and everything in between for the rotten luck. Ida and Vellora stood in the crowd, though no one seemed to be doing anything about filling in the sinkhole.

"Inn is okay," Ida said before Bev could even ask. "You look filthy. What have you been doing all day? Rolling in the dirt?"

"In a manner of speaking," Bev said with a heavy sigh. "I found the gnomes. They say they aren't doing this."

"And you believe those queen's ass-kissing fiends?" Vellora asked.

Bev lifted a shoulder, not wanting to get into an argument with her. But as she dropped her gaze, she noticed the muddiness of her boots. But that wasn't from her trip down into the mines; it was from stepping in the mud outside Trent Scrawl's property. Mud that, based on the lack of rain lately, shouldn't have been there.

Now, Bev wasn't about to embark on conspiracy theories, but…but something told her that was the next thing she needed to investigate.

CHAPTER EIGHT

"Really, I'm sure Trent Scrawl has nothing to do with any of this," Bev muttered to herself as she scrubbed the inside of her large iron pot in the middle of her chores. The night before, she'd whipped up the fastest Emergency Vegetable Stew in history—a good thing because Etheldra, Earl, and Gore Dewey all came to eat. She'd barely engaged them in conversation, too focused on Trent Scrawl's muddy farm and the gnome's words.

All night long, she'd tossed and turned, thinking and rethinking.

After all, what did mud prove? Nothing.

Except that there was water. Water coming from

somewhere it didn't need to be.

But the gnomes had said river. *And the only thing low was the Pigsend Creek. How specific were they, anyway?*

Bev argued with herself over whether she should discard an entire idea over word choice—especially as there certainly *was* something suspicious about Trent. His pumpkin was huge, his wheat fields had been quite lush for the dry weather this late in the season. But perhaps he just had the green thumb others lacked. He'd been called out by Herman Monday, but that was just professional jealousy and nothing more.

"Don't be ridiculous, Bev," she muttered as she scrubbed a particularly baked-on piece of potato. "He wouldn't have done anything to hurt the town."

But he would do whatever it took to show up Herman Monday in the Harvest Festival.

She stopped and sat up straight. Now *that* was a thought worth investigating. Ida had said their rivalry went back decades. The Harvest Festival was the height of the social calendar in Pigsend, so wouldn't it be something if Trent showed up with a pumpkin that dwarfed everyone else's?

This was an itch that needed to be scratched. With a sigh, she pulled off her apron and wiped her hands, gazing around her kitchen and deciding it was clean enough for the moment. She could go down to Trent's house, check things out, make *sure* she hadn't dreamed the mud on her boots, then be back in time to start dinner.

"Just a quick walk," she whispered to herself. "Nothing suspicious. I'm allowed to walk down the road."

Still, her pulse quickened as she approached the farm. The last thing she wanted was to unnecessarily stir the pot. She got along fine with most everyone in Pigsend (save, apparently, Allen Mackey). Besides that, as of now, there was nothing to stir. So why was she so nervous?

Luckily, Trent was in his back fields, too absorbed in feeding his goats to notice her. She exhaled nervously, walking briskly toward the fields where she'd seen the mud the day before, near his pumpkin patch.

There it was. A trickle of wet dirt that seemed to spill from the thick patch of wheat that lined the fence. Bev closed her eyes, said a small prayer, then hopped the fence into the wheat.

She winced as her feet squelched in the mud, but Trent was too far to hear anyway. Slowly, she pushed the wheat plants out of the way as she made her way over to the pumpkin patch. His gourd was impressive, even from a distance, but it wasn't the only one. He had no fewer than seven big, orange globes sitting amidst the tangle of vines. Any one of them could be a contender at the Harvest Festival.

On the ground next to them—a small fountain of water spurting up from the ground.

"What in the..." She was bending down to inspect it when she heard the unmistakable sound of footfalls approaching. Panicking, Bev dove into the thicket of wheat and held her breath.

"Just look at ya," Trent said, standing in front of his pumpkin. "I..." He frowned, gazing at the ground beside the pumpkin.

Bev realized with a start that her footprints were probably still visible.

"That sneaky little..." he growled.

Bev bit her lip, ready to confess.

"Herman Monday! You are gonna hear it from me!" he called to the open air. "If I see you skulking around my prize pumpkin again, I'm gonna rip out your whole garden and feed it to my goats, you hear?"

Bev waited for him to come into the wheat plants, but he just let out a loud huff and stalked away.

She waited a few breaths before walking back toward the road. This had been a *terrible* idea. Why'd she been so keen to come out here in the first place? Large pumpkins? Water on the ground? Silly stuff. Not that Trent would do much more than be cross at her if he found her in his plants, but still.

And yet, as she stood in the road, the farm contrasted with the dusty, dry world beyond. He was getting water from somewhere—and Bev had to think he hadn't just stumbled upon a nice underground pond. It was too much of a coincidence, especially with Pigsend Creek being so low.

Maybe the creek is back up.

It was just across the road from Trent's farm, so she quickly made her way toward the rushing water. Or rather…the small trickle. It should've been at least knee-high, filled with fish, frogs, and birds splashing about in the water. But it was eerily silent today.

Far off in town, the bell tower clanged to signal noon, and Bev sighed. She needed to get back to the inn and finish chores, not to mention check on her guests. Although they hadn't really been the most needy of tenants, they seemed to put a cloud over the town, and she'd be happy when they moved on.

~

Unfortunately, Bev found another five coins waiting on the front desk and couldn't help but scowl. Another night with her soldier friends. And she was plum out of most everything in the kitchen, which meant she'd have to high-tail it to the farmers' market before it closed—and perhaps talk with Herman Monday about his feud with Trent Scrawl.

But as she walked out the back door, she stopped short. Allen Mackey's flour remained on Bev's wagon.

She huffed, turning to walk across the street *again*, and this time, she wasn't going to take no for an answer. She didn't try the front door, instead walking around to the back and banging on the back door.

"Allen Mackey, if you don't open this door right now, I will break it down—or I'll get Ida to, so—"

The door opened and Allen's meek face appeared. There were dark circles under his eyes and he seemed even more pale than usual. "What is it, Bev?"

"Why haven't you come to get your flour?" she asked. "Are you sick?"

"Yes." He coughed into his hand, but it was clearly fake. "Very sick. Now leave me alone."

He tried to shut the door, but she wedged her boot in the crack. "Don't slam your door on me, kid. Now, your sweet mother got me started across the street, and I promised myself I'd look after her boy when she passed. If you're in some kind of trouble, or if you need help, you know I'm here for you—"

"I don't need your help, and I don't need you meddling in my business." He kicked her foot out of the door. "Now leave me alone, you stupid old hag."

He slammed the door and Bev's eyes widened as it nearly hit her in the face. She took a step back, unsure what to do next. She turned, looking for Allen's cart, and saw it sitting against the empty stables.

Wait, empty?

Bev walked over to the stable, searching for the Mackeys' trusty horse Penelope. But she was nowhere to be found. And based on the muck on top of the water, it seemed that she hadn't been there in quite some time. No wonder Allen hadn't gone to get his flour. Without a horse to pull the cart, how was he supposed to transport his baking supplies? Penelope wasn't old by any stretch, which meant… He'd probably sold her. For what purpose, Bev didn't quite know, but it added to an already troubling picture of the young man.

"Oh, Allen, what are you doing, kid?" she said with a sigh, looking up at the bakery.

But Allen's problems would have to wait. Bev had precious little time to get ready for dinner, and she doubted that vegetable stew would fly for the third night in a row.

Sin seemed eager to get out of her pen, and happily pulled Allen's wagon down the road. Bev hadn't asked if she could borrow it; it seemed that Allen wouldn't even notice it was missing. He did have a hand cart, but she wasn't about to push ten pounds of potatoes an hour down the road.

As Bev exited town, she passed the very first sinkhole. As before, it was difficult to maneuver Sin and the cart around the gaping hole in the road. If anything, it looked *bigger* than before, though Bev didn't have a measuring stick or anything like that. It made her worry about the sinkhole in front of the inn, and how many more earthquakes it would take before it swallowed the building whole.

Yet, here you are, going to the farmers' market instead of...

Instead of what? Traipsing around Trent Scrawl's property looking for trouble?

But as they traveled down the dirt road, it was impossible to ignore the brown, dying fields outside town. It was different crops for sure—the farmers near to the mill tended to grow more wheat and this side of town was more produce and cotton—but the corn stalks should have still been green, the rows of low-lying vegetable plants were withered and dry, even the grape vines looked to be struggling. The grass that lined the road was a dark, scraggly brown, too.

Yet Trent Scrawl's property was…*thriving*.

"Stop trying to make trouble from nothing," she muttered.

The farmers on this side of town held market twice a week, their stands usually overflowing with whatever was in season. But from the looks of things, the fields were an accurate reflection of the current crop.

"Sorry for the selection, Bev," Grant Klose said with a shake of his head as she approached his stand. "I think last week's was the tail end of the good stuff. We'll be in a pickle for fall if we don't get some rain soon."

"I'll be keeping my hopes up for you," she said, handing over a gold coin for the last of his rutabagas and potatoes.

She moved on to Alice Estrich, who had a large orchard of different fruits. Her apples looked a bit small and puny, but they'd cook up just fine into a sauce to go with the pork she was planning on buying from Vellora and Ida. Another gold coin for three bushels that she loaded up on Allen's cart.

Finally, Bev approached Herman Monday's stand. Like the others, he wore a look of disdain as she inspected the carrots and beets.

"I don't know what's going on," he said with a shake of his head. "It's like everything's just up and died overnight. It's all I can do to keep my Harvest

Festival pumpkin watered and fed."

Bev put the best-looking of the bunch into her satchel. "I know it's been tough lately, what with the lack of rain—"

"Not just rain," Herman said. "Something *foul* is afoot. All these earthquakes? No rain?" He shook his head. "Those gnomes are probably up to no good. Glad you're giving them the what-for."

Bev ducked her gaze. "Hopefully, they'll move on soon." She poked his produce a bit before asking, "Say, have you been up to see Trent Scrawl's land lately?"

He glared at Bev so hard that she almost cowered in fear. "I try to avoid the devil if I can."

"True story," she said with a nervous smile. "I just… He seems to be doing well with his crops this year. I wondered if you'd heard anything about that?"

"If he is, it's because he's a no-good cheater."

"How…" She cleared her throat. "How does one 'cheat' at farming?"

"I don't know. Magic or something. But I swear he's got it!" The old man's face was now bright red as he prattled on. "But joke's on him. I've been pumping water out of the ground to make sure *my* entry for the Harvest Festival is gonna win!" He lifted his chin. "I bet you it'll be my biggest pumpkin to date."

Bev couldn't help but chuckle. "So instead of watering the crops that earn you money, you're using your water to make sure you get bragging rights?"

Another death glare and Bev casually slid over a gold coin. "I'll just take the carrots and beets, thank you."

Bev left the market shortly after that, her mind racing with thoughts, theories, ideas. So much so that had Sin not brayed angrily, she would have led them right into the sinkhole in the middle of the road.

"Sorry old girl," Bev said, getting down off the cart. "Mind's elsewhere."

They maneuvered around once more, and Bev's mind went back to wandering. If she *were* to investigate again, it might be best to do it later this evening. She could cook and serve dinner like normal then head out after dark. Trent would be asleep, so she could really have a look around without worrying about him seeing her.

Great, now you're planning to skulk.

But Trent probably wouldn't entertain questions, especially if it had anything to do with his prized gourd.

"Oi!" Sheriff Rustin waved at her from atop a mound nearby. "How goes the investigation?"

"Got some threads I'm pulling," she said. "The gnomes were a dead end, unfortunately."

He frowned. "Are they really? All of them?"

She pursed her lips to keep a smile off her face. "Dead *end*, not dead, Rustin. They said they aren't involved."

"Oh, right, right, right, right." He nodded. "Sorry, been a bit frazzled lately. The queen's soldiers have me running all over the place, you know." He rubbed the back of his head. "Any chance they've told you how long they're in town?"

"No, but they've paid for another night, so they're here until tomorrow at least," Bev said, nodding to the back of her cart. "So I figure I might as well make dinner. You're welcome to come, though they haven't really been all that willing to eat with the rest of us. Don't know if you'll be able to have a good chat with them."

"I've had enough chats with them," he said. "Lately, they've had me standing guard up here on the road to the dark forest." He nodded to the thick growth of trees on the far eastern part of town that was best avoided at all costs. "No idea why. Just told me to keep any townsfolk away from them."

Bev nodded, wondering if the sheriff had deterred Allen any. "I'm sure they'll be on their way soon enough."

"So this thread you're pulling on for the

sinkholes," Rustin said. "Care to share what it is? Can I help?"

Bev hesitated. Should she tell the sole law enforcement officer in town she would basically be trespassing to follow a hunch that might or might not come to fruition?

"I don't think I need any help quite yet—still trying to wrap my head around what's going on," she said with what she hoped was a genuine smile. "But if I do, I'll be sure to find you." She turned toward the sinkhole. "If you're looking for something to—*ahem*—keep you out of town, you might see about filling in that sinkhole so nobody falls in."

"Right. That sounds like a plan." He beamed. "Thanks, Bev."

"Have a good one, Rustin."

As she rolled away, she couldn't help but feel like she was *already* breaking the law, and she hadn't even set one foot on Trent Scrawl's property.

CHAPTER NINE

Tonight's dinner was to be a simple pork roast with apples, roasted beets, and potatoes she'd gotten from the farmers. As she sliced up the root vegetables, she kept thinking about how puny they appeared, and how very lush Trent's farm was. In fact, she was so engrossed in her thoughts she barely heard the knock at the back door.

"Dinner still served if we come in this way?" Bardoff poked his head in. "Smells great, Bev."

"Oh, yeah," she said with a smile. "Just about ready."

"Any rosemary bread tonight?" Etheldra asked, walking inside with a haughty expression.

"No, sorry. I've been a bit preoccupied," Bev said, picking up the platter of meat and walking it into the dining room. "Soon, I hope."

"Harrumph."

"Oh, be nice, Etheldra," Bardoff said. "Bev's not the resident baker in town, you know."

"Yeah, but Allen's baking leaves a lot to be desired," Etheldra grumbled, grabbing a plate and loading herself up.

Earl showed up soon after, and Bev sat behind the counter at the front desk, toying with the quill as she kept a wary eye on the clock. Would Trent be asleep yet? She assumed farmers didn't keep late hours.

"Bev."

She jumped. "What?"

"I said, this pork is to *die* for," Earl said, taking another huge bite in his mouth. "Whaf dif ew puf im it?"

"Just some herbs from the garden," she said, glancing at the clock on the wall again and putting down the quill before she tore up the feather.

"Bev?"

"Yes, what?" she said, borderline snapping. Etheldra quirked a brow, and she softened. "Sorry. What can I do for you?"

"I just wanted to know if you solved the mystery yet?" Etheldra asked. "Give those no-good gnomes the boot?"

"Ah, unfortunately, no," she said, picking up the quill again then putting it down. "They said they're not responsible."

The table went quiet as three dubious faces looked at her.

"And you believed them?" Earl said.

"Well, of course I did," Bev said. "Why would they lie?"

"Because they're sneaky little magical creatures," Earl said. "There's a reason the queen eradicated most of them."

"The queen likes these guys though," Bev said. "They did give me some ideas on who or what might be causing it. I don't want to say until I know for sure, though."

"Better hurry," Bardoff said. "The next sinkhole might actually hurt someone. We've been very lucky so far that none have."

"Hear, hear," Etheldra said.

"If this particular hunch doesn't pan out," Bev said, "I'll pay them another visit. Promise." She rose from the table, undoing her apron as she could no longer sit still and wait for the clock to tick. "And if you three will be so kind as to drop your dirty dishes in the sink when you're done, I'm going to look into this particular idea."

"At night?" Bardoff said.

"Must be someone in town," Etheldra said with a deliciously sinister look. "I hope you catch them red-handed. We could use some more gossip."

"It's not someone in town," Bev said, which was technically true. "And there's no gossip to be had here, Etheldra, you know that."

"Pshaw." Etheldra scowled. "You'd better hurry up and solve this, because I'm getting impatient for that bread of yours."

"Mm." Bev waved them off. "Have a good night."

The night was quiet, and Bev headed toward the stables where the five horses for the soldiers were sleeping. One woke up and neighed at her angrily, and she shushed him, even though it wasn't out of the ordinary for Bev to be in her *own* stable. But every move she made felt like a trespass, even the breaths she took as she searched through the dark closet.

"Come on. I know you're here somewhere," she whispered.

Finally, her hand closed around a long stick stuffed between a spare rake and shovel. She pulled it toward her, squinting in the scant light to make sure it was the right stick. Small mushrooms grew on the top of it, and when she was out in the starlight, they offered a nice glow that helped her see in the dark. It had come in handy when Stella's old dog had gotten loose and they'd had to comb the countryside for him. And, perhaps tonight, it would come in handy as Bev snuck around Trent Scrawl's property.

She lowered the stick and sighed. What in the world was she doing?

Saving the Weary Dragon Inn, came the clear response from her mind.

The moment she stepped into the night sky, the mushrooms illuminated softly, allowing her to at least see the steps in front of her, and Bev walked toward the east, and Trent's home. Ida and Vellora still had a light on in their apartment above the butcher shop, but there weren't many others who did. Almost everyone was asleep—except Bev, it seemed.

Every step she took felt like another infraction. She was allowed to be out at night; there wasn't a curfew in town. But it all just felt so dangerous she couldn't help but move quietly as she left the town behind and started out on the road through the farmlands. Trent's was perhaps a thirty-minute walk from the inn—not that Bev was in any hurry to get there.

She stopped short. Something moved in a small thicket of trees near the road. She lifted the glowing stick higher. "Hello?"

More movement, but no response.

Could it be a wild animal? Probably. Just a wild animal.

Bev exhaled and kept walking when she heard voices.

She turned around, walking toward the forest with her heart thumping wildly.

"Hello?" Bev called again, using her glow stick to move a branch out of the way. "Is someone in there?"

A shadow moved quickly, and Bev cried out in surprise. But the glow stick reflected off the shiny queens-pin on the soldier, who spun at Bev with a wild look on his face. It was one of the four nameless soldiers who followed Karolina. He had something long and black in his hands pointed at the ground. He gave Bev a once-over, his expression shifting from surprise to suspicion to disgust in mere seconds.

"What are you doing out here so late, innkeeper?" he practically spat at her.

"Just...out for a nightly walk," Bev said, hoping that sounded convincing. "What about you?"

"Conducting busbusiness," he said, straightening. "Business which does not concern you. I suggest you return to your inn for the night."

"Understood," Bev said, taking a step back. "Well, um...carry on, I guess. The back door to the inn is open if—"

"Good *night*, innkeeper."

The finality of his tone was clear, and Bev simply nodded and kept walking. She cast a wary look behind her as the soldier walked back into the brush but decided not to investigate further. The sooner the soldiers finished their secretive work, the better.

She kept walking down the dark road and didn't hear another soul, save the crickets and frogs that lived in the forested areas near the road. The sound was rather soothing and eased some of Bev's nerves. But as she came closer to Trent's property, her pulse spiked again.

She stood on the road for a moment, gazing at his farmhouse in the distance. There weren't any lights on, so at least he was asleep. That didn't do much to make her feel better.

With a grunt, she hopped over the fence into his front fields. It was a little hard to remember where everything was in the dark, and the ground was hard and dry. She lowered the glowing stick so she could see where to put her feet, and illuminated a knotted mass of gourd vines.

"Should be close," she whispered, walking forward along the fence line. But it was hard to keep the stick near the ground, so she straightened and kept it in front of her.

Something large and soft caught the tip of her

boot, and Bev nearly fell on her hands and knees. For a brief, terrifying moment, she worried she might've damaged the beautiful pumpkin that Trent had so eagerly been protecting. But it didn't feel like a pumpkin, in fact, it felt like…

She lowered the glowing stick and had to bite her lip to keep from laughing. Trent was sleeping on the ground, curled around his prized pumpkin. He hadn't woken, so Bev carefully inched backward and kept the light behind her so it wouldn't rouse him. Back, back, back she crept until she was a safe distance away—and landed in a field of thick wheat.

She took a stalk in her hand and touched the grain head. As predicted, it was healthy, full of life. Not at all like the rest of the farmlands in the surrounding area. She turned to keep walking, looking for something that might give away Trent's secret.

Her toe hit something else—this time low and hard. She knelt closer with the glow stick.

"A metal pipe?" she whispered. "What in the…"

It came out of the ground just a bit, and as she ran her fingers along the top, she felt small holes that had been drilled into the pipe. It emerged from the ground maybe six inches in length before falling back under the dirt. She followed the prospective path, pushing aside the wheat as she crept along until another emerged from the ground. Same story

—roughly six inches of metal pipe that had holes drilled into it. On and on she followed it, through the field until she reached the fencing.

Trent's house was to her left, which meant the Pigsend Creek was just over the road and through the thicket on the other side.

So…that explained it.

Bev had to laugh. Vicky would have a field day when she found out. She'd warned of all sorts of problems if Pigsend Creek was diverted, and clearly…she'd been right.

But Bev wouldn't know for sure until she found the evidence in the creek, so with care, she hopped the fence and headed toward it. The brambles in the thicket tugged and pulled at her clothes, and she wished she'd worn taller boots. Then again, she wasn't used to skulking, so perhaps *next time* she'd know better.

The thicket left scratches all along her arms, but finally, Bev landed in what should've been the creek. It was still *very* low but actually a little higher than before. Then again, Trent didn't seem to be siphoning off water at the moment.

She brought her glowing stick toward the water, running her hands along the shallow creek bed. It was muddy, full of rocks, and she might've felt the occasional something dead that sent a spiral of squick up her arm. She looked back at the thicket, trying to stay relatively close.

Ahead, there was a small puddle of water, almost like a pond in the middle of the dry creek bed. A large rock was poking out, leaning up against the side of the bank—although not strange on its own, it just *looked* out of place, half-submerged as it was.

Bev inspected the stone as best she could over the small pond. It was loose, so she pulled it forward, letting it splash in the reservoir and revealing a dark hole. The end of Trent's illegal pipe. Almost immediately, the water drained down the now-open pipe as quickly as it could—pulling more water from the already-low creek behind it.

Not a minute later came Trent's horrified yelp in the distance. She turned quickly, rushing back to his farm.

She came into the clearing, her stick held aloft, as Trent cursed and complained. Beside him, there was a spray of water—the river water Bev had just let back in the pipes.

"Son of a—" He turned, spotting her standing in the middle of road. "Bev? Is that you? What in tarnation are you doing out here at this time of night?"

Bev had a choice. She could say nothing—take her findings to Rustin and the rest of the town and let them deal with Trent Scrawl in their own way. Or...or she could do the farmer a favor and let him know what he was doing to the town.

"How long have you been draining the river to water your crops, Trent?" she asked quietly.

"I'm not… This isn't…"

"I found your little pipe," Bev said. "You're the only farmer in fifty miles who's had a good fall crop. Don't take me for a fool."

His shoulders dropped. "What are you gonna do? Tell the sheriff?" He wrung his hands. "Tell the committee at the Harvest Festival? It's just water, I tell you. Nothing more than that."

"And you draining the river has been causing sinkholes," Bev said.

"It… What?" He snapped his head up. "That's impossible. I've been doing it for months now!"

Bev licked her lips. *Months?* "Maybe with the drought, it finally came to a head. Regardless, you need to cut it out. Sonny's been complaining that he barely has enough water to push the mill and the rest of us need the creek, too. You can't just keep all the water for yourself so you can have the biggest pumpkin in the patch. It's not fair, and it's not right. You know that."

She'd expected more of a fight, but the old farmer nodded.

"Now, let's go plug the hole—for *good*," Bev said.

Bev and Trent returned to the riverside and covered the hole with the rock. Trent watched it sadly before finally following Bev back to his property. In the walk back to his property, Bev found herself feeling sorry for the farmer, even though he'd caused more trouble than he was worth.

"You know," Bev said, after a long pause, "I think that pumpkin is plenty big. I was just up at Herman Monday's farm earlier today. Everything on his land is deader than dead. I'm sure your pumpkin still stands a chance to beat his—even without the creek."

"Maybe we'll get some rain to keep helping things along?" he said, looking up. "Say Bev, I appreciate you…keeping this between us. Can't tell you how troublesome it'd be to have Rustin sniffing around here. And for what it's worth, I had no clue the dry river caused the sinkholes." He shook his head. "Who gave you that idea?"

"The gnomes, actually."

He scoffed. "They would say that. Anything to keep suspicion off them, you know."

"Trent, the creek is practically gone," Bev said, gesturing toward the river. "It makes sense."

"If you say so." He huffed. "Better hope it rains."

"For all our sakes, yes." The lateness of the night

finally came for her as she fought off a yawn. "I'm headed back to town. Got lots to do at the inn in the morning now that we've solved this problem. But if I hear of the river getting low again, and see your stone's overturned, I will be telling Rustin." She paused. "And the Harvest Festival committee *and* Herman Monday."

"You wouldn't dare tell that old badger!" Trent gasped.

"As long as you keep your word," Bev said, "I'll keep mine."

CHAPTER TEN

Two days passed. There wasn't another earthquake in the area, and the sinkholes didn't grow any bigger. To boot, a massive storm blew through town, practically dumping rain for hours. Bev watched the deluge from her window, smiling as she sipped a cup of tea and thought about how Trent Scrawl had gotten lucky after all. When there was a break in the weather, Bev ventured down to the creek close to town and was pleased to see it higher than it had been in weeks. True to her word, she didn't tell a soul about Trent's illegal water poaching, but she did go to the river to make sure the rock was still where she'd left it.

When she returned to the inn, the back door was open and there was a trail of mud leading through the kitchen to the front desk. There stood the five soldiers, including the one Bev had run into on her evening adventure to Trent's house. He was doing his best to avoid looking at Bev.

"Innkeeper," Karolina barked. "We are in need of your services."

"Of course. What can I do for you?" Bev said, sliding onto the stool behind the desk.

"We require our clothes to be laundered," she said. "We will leave them outside our door and expect them to be washed, dried, and folded by the time we depart this evening."

"Oh, you guys are leaving?" Bev said, almost a little hopefully.

"No." She lifted her chin. "We're not finished with our business."

Bev glanced behind Karolina to the dark gray sky above. "I'll do my best, but the weather might not—"

"That will be all, innkeeper." She slapped ten gold coins down on the table before walking away.

Bev pulled the money toward herself, intending to tell the soldier that it only cost a silver per for laundry, but deciding against it. If they had the queen's gold to spend, Bev wasn't about to say otherwise.

They turned to march up the stairs, leaving a trail of black mud behind them. Bev sighed—she'd just mopped and swept earlier that morning. She heard the telltale sound of five doors opening and closing then clothing being deposited outside the door. She waited until she counted five separate door slams before pushing herself off the stool and walking up the stairs.

She shook her head and kept to the side of the muddy footprints, though she stopped when she noticed the shimmer of orange dust mixed in the mud.

Strange.

In the hallway of the second floor, there were five disorganized piles in front of the doors, so Bev took care to keep them separate as she brought them downstairs. They were all exactly the same, but Bev had a feeling if she put one sock out of place, she'd hear about it. And as much of a pain in the butt as these soldiers were, she could still hear ol' Wim's voice in her head reminding her to always be generous and kind, even in the face of spite.

She dragged her wash basin from its spot near the kitchen back door toward the pump and pumped out some water. Unlike the previous few weeks, water was plentiful—another good sign that perhaps things were back to normal.

That strange orange dust that had been in their

footprints also covered their clothing—and Bev was having trouble placing what, exactly, it was. More powdery than the rest of the dirt, it sat on top of the water as Bev scrubbed the clothes in the wash basin. In fact, she had to dump her suds bucket three or four times while washing just to get all of it off.

"It's bad enough they're staying here. Now I gotta look at their colors?" Vellora rounded the corner with a frown. She had the three pork loins Bev had ordered hanging from a stick. "Gross."

"They aren't here. Don't worry," Bev said. "Or they're sleeping. Can't quite figure out their schedule."

"I'd say not, with your traipsing about trying to solve the sinkhole problem," Vellora said. "Will you have time to cook this tonight?"

"Hopefully," Bev said, dusting her hands off and standing up. "Have you ever seen this orange powder around?"

"Can't say I have," Vellora said, shaking her head.

"Hm." Bev dumped another bucket of water. "Well, they're clean now, anyway. Perhaps that might improve their dispositions. I swear they haven't said three words to me since they arrived, other than to bark orders."

"That's what they do," Vellora said. She was starting to look uncomfortable standing in the middle of the laundry line of Queenside soldiers. "Um… I have to be getting back to Ida, you know."

"Oh, right!" Bev hopped up and took the pork from her. "Thank you for dropping it off."

"I see Allen hasn't come to collect his flour yet," she said as she turned to leave. Bev's cart was still sitting where it had been for the past three days, the blanket draped over the five sacks of flour, untouched, though the tarp had kept most of the rain off it. "Then again, I haven't seen a single customer come in or out of his bakery in a few days, either."

Bev nodded. "Something strange is going on with that boy, but he sure won't tell me about it. Practically slammed the door in my face the other day."

"If he doesn't come to collect, you should just keep it and use the flour to make some delicious rosemary bread," Vellora said. "Not that I'm hankering for a loaf or anything…"

"Let me get my sinkhole filled," Bev said. "And then I'll make two loaves just for you and Ida."

Dawn broke on the third day since the appearance of any sinkholes, and Bev began to feel confident the worst was behind the town of Pigsend. It was time to get things back to normal, and that included filling the hole outside her front door. The

Harvest Festival was coming up in the next month, and she didn't fancy having all her guests traipse through the back door of the inn.

She walked out her back door, staring at her cart that was *still* laden with flour. She very well could have just kept it—she'd paid for it after all—but that just didn't sit right with her. It was Allen's, and she just wanted it off her hands.

So with a smile on her face, she crossed the other side to the butcher shop and poked her head in.

"Morning, Ida, dear."

Ida was wiping the counter while humming a unique melody and grinned when the bell tinkled above Bev's head. "What can I do for you today, Bev? Thinking it's a nice night for some pork shank?"

"That does sound good, but I was hoping I might borrow you for a minute or two," Bev said. "Since Allen won't come get his stuff, I need some help bringing it to him."

She sighed. "You know, I'm more than just muscle, Bev."

Bev straightened. "Of course I know that, Ida, you're—"

"Oh, I'm just kidding," she said with a giggle. "Of course, I'll help you. Let me just let the missus know I'm stepping out."

Roping in Ida was a good idea. Bev was only able to hoist one ten-pound sack on her shoulder, while Ida threw the remaining four on either shoulder. Bev marveled at how the lithe woman was able to handle so much, but as usual, she didn't want to pry.

"I wonder what's up with the kid anyway," Ida said as they crossed the street. "I've seen poor Vicky hovering around his back door. Maybe they had a lovers' quarrel."

"And how long has *that* been going on?" Bev asked, huffing and puffing under the weight. "I consider myself a nosy neighbor and had no clue the two of them were sweet on each other."

"Oh, it's still in the 'will they, won't they' phase," Ida said. "Vicky might be a little too…" She cast a nervous look around. "Flighty for Allen. He's pretty stable. Normally, anyway."

They rapped on the door, but no one answered, so they left the sacks on the back step.

"I wish there was something to cover them with," Bev said. "Maybe I should go grab the tarp from—"

"Oh, just let it be," Ida said. "You've done more than he deserves, I'll tell you that much."

And Ida didn't even know that Bev had paid for the flour. Still, her heart tugged for the kid, and she had the funds to do it.

"Well, at least I've got my cart back so I can see about filling the sinkhole," Bev said, eager to change the subject.

"Did you finally tell those gnomes off?" Ida asked as they headed back across the street.

"Actually..." Bev smiled. "Can you keep a secret?"

"You know I can." She leaned in. "Especially if it's juicy."

Bev told her about Trent Scrawl and the wet spots near his property, finding the pipes he'd laid and how it had all but drained the river.

"The gnomes said something was disrupting the river," Bev said. "And since he's stopped draining the river, the earthquakes have stopped, right?"

The words themselves almost summoned the earth to move. Bev and Ida scrambled to hang onto something before they both fell to their knees. The rumbling was intense and lasted a full three minutes or so. Once the ground stopped moving, Bev and Ida hopped to their feet and dashed toward their respective homes.

The inn looked fine, though there were a few more cracks in the ground near the front door. Bev heaved a sigh of relief and scanned the immediate area for where the sinkhole could've occurred.

"Help, help!"

Bev turned on her heel and ran toward the

voice, which sounded like Shasta Brewer. The twins lived the next street over—or had. There was a giant hole where their house used to be.

"Help!" Shasta cried, tears streaming down her face. "My sister's in there!"

Bev ran toward the hole, but Ida was faster, jumping down and moving big pieces of wall and wood like they were toothpicks. A couple others came to help, including Jane and Earl, but their attempts were paltry compared to Ida's quick work.

Vicky had her arms wrapped around the distraught twin, who was biting her nails as the minutes ticked by. But after a moment, she straightened, shock turning to a smile.

"She's alive!" Shasta called. "There! To the left!"

Ida turned and pulled a rather large piece of brick wall off the ground, tossing it away. Underneath, curled under an enormous iron pot, was Stella Brewer. She had a nasty bruise on her forehead and was bleeding, but as Ida helped her stand, she looked otherwise unharmed.

"Help her up!" Bev called, reaching down into the hole for the twin.

Earl and Jane took her by the arms and held her aloft, and Bev and Vicky hoisted her out. They sat her on the ground, and Shasta ran over, throwing her arms around her sister and dissolving into sobs.

"I'm…okay…" Stella said, weakly. "Just a little

dizzy."

"Does anyone know if Doc Howser's in town this week?" Bev asked. The local healer did a rotation between the surrounding villages, but he was never more than a few hours away.

Vicky shook her head. "I think he's down the road in Sheepsberg."

"Can we send someone to fetch him?"

She jumped up. "I'll find someone."

She dashed away as Vellora brought a wet rag smelling of ale to clean up Stella's wounds. "This may sting a little, but it'll keep the infections out until we can get you to Howser."

"Clear the way, clear the way!" Mayor Hendry parted the crowd with just her voice as she ran over to survey the damage. Her sharp gaze landed on the Brewer twin, and she hurried over, kneeling next to her. "Dear Stella, goodness me, what happened?"

"Sinkhole," Shasta spoke for her sister, glaring evilly at Bev. "Since they're still a thing, apparently."

"Has anyone fetched Doc Howser yet?" Hendry asked.

"Just now," Vellora replied.

"Well, then, in the meantime, why don't we get you into my office? You can lie down on my couch until he arrives." Hendry gingerly helped Stella to her feet. "There now, let's just go slowly. No need to rush."

Stella limped away, bolstered by her sister and the mayor. Bev sighed as they disappeared down the street, wishing she had better answers.

"Suppose you'd better go back to those gnomes and give them a talking to," Ida said, coming up beside Bev as she wiped dirt from her face. "Maybe bring a large stick this time."

Bev marched straight back to the gnomes' nest, balancing anger with rationality. She'd always been a good judge of character, had good gut feelings about people, and other than her being brushed off as obnoxious, the gnomes had seemed cordial enough. They'd gotten the foreman; he'd spoken to her.

Unless, of course, it had all been one big diversion.

She balled her fists as she marched over the final hill, ready with a tirade of complaints at the tiny creatures when she stopped short.

They were…gone.

What had days ago been a dusty, dirty worksite was now a verdant hill covered in long, flowing grass. The heliotrope and pink fountain grass that had led Bev to the gnomes originally were mixed in, of course, but it was hard to tell that there'd been a gnome worksite here at all.

Bev glanced behind her, making sure she'd taken the right path. She had—she was sure of it.

Slowly, she walked down into the valley, kneeling in search of some evidence that she hadn't dreamed the entire encounter. Running her hands along the grass, she found nothing, nothing, nothing until...her fingers made purchase on something small.

A discarded boot. One of the gnome's.

They had been here. How long they'd been gone was anybody's guess, but clearly, they'd meant it when they said they left things as they found them.

And also, she realized with a start, if they were gone, she could no longer ask them about the guidance they'd given her. The river was full, the gnomes were gone, and it seemed...it seemed the investigation had come to a dead end. Not the sort of news that would make anyone in town happy with her.

She got to her feet, knowing it would be better to get the news out of the way sooner rather than later, when the ground began to shake again. It wasn't nearly as bad as the earlier earthquake, more like a tremor. The ground in front of her pulsed and she took three steps back, ready to run for her life.

Finally, the bulging gave way and a gigantic mole came bursting from the ground, climbing out with a huff and brushing his whiskers off with his paws.

"Good, I thought I heard someone up here," he

said, his voice low and scratchy. "Now, who do I need to talk with about all these darn earthquakes ruining my home?"

CHAPTER ELEVEN

Bev stared at the creature, who shook to rid himself of the dirt, and could scarcely believe her eyes. Sure, the gnomes had been a bit odd to look at, but this...this was a *giant mole*. He was almost the size of Vellora, yet rounder and covered in black fur from head to toe...er...paw. His eyes were almost invisible. His snout was bright pink, and his claws were long and sharp.

His whiskers shook when he spoke, which he did eloquently, and he sat on his haunches as he addressed her. "Excuse me? I'm talking to you," he said. "Do you understand me?"

"Uh, yes. Yes, of course," Bev said with a

nervous clearing of her throat. "What did you say?"

"I asked you," he took a step toward her, unsticking the claws on his feet from the ground, "if you topsiders would *kindly* quit doing whatever it is you're doing that's causing all these confounded earthquakes!"

"We aren't..." Bev shook her head, her mind finally catching up with the rest of her. "No, that's not what we're doing. You're the one who just caused an earthquake!"

He chuckled. "And why in the world would I do something to further endanger my home? I've already lost an entire wall to this incessant shaking."

She frowned. "Your home? You live here?"

"Of course I do!" he said with a jovial sort of tone. "I've been here for nearly half a century."

"But I've never seen you in town," Bev said. "I've never seen anything like you before..."

Again, he chuckled. "I wouldn't be coming to your town, topsider. The sun is harsh, and I prefer the quiet of my hearth and chair." He tilted his head. "Surely, you have some idea about these earthquakes, hm? Something new, something changed. Something different?"

Bev gestured to the hill where the heliotropes and fountain grass were blooming. "The gnomes that were here told me one thing, but it seems that wasn't right. And now they're gone." She kicked the grass, annoyed. "Maybe everyone in town was right. Maybe they did cause them."

"Well, goodness me," the mole said. "I don't love those greedy magic excavators, but they're good stewards of the land. They know more about what goes on under the surface than most. Whatever they told you, I'm sure, was right."

"Except I fixed it, and the problem remains," Bev said, a little impatiently.

"Then perhaps you misunderstood them," he offered. "You know, I've got some knowledge of how the ground sits and shifts, being a digger myself. And I find the best ideas come from a cuppa and a nice cozy fire. Why don't you come with me, and we can chat out of this hot sun?"

"Come with you…where?" Bev asked, looking around.

"To my home, of course!" He actually looked like he was smiling. "It's not that far. Come, come."

He turned to dive into the hole he'd climbed out of. Bev looked left then right. Following a mole creature into a dark hole seemed like a bad idea, but despite his long claws, he seemed rather harmless. Besides that, a creature that spent all his time underground might have some insights Bev didn't, so it was worth a shot to hear him out.

The mole reappeared, waving at her again. "Hurry up. We haven't got all day."

With a shrug, she hopped into the hole and followed the path the mole had dug.

The incline was steep, and once or twice, she almost slipped and fell, but eventually, the angle leveled out. The mushrooms Bev used on her glowing stick were prevalent along this path. The mole was far ahead, but every so often, he'd stop to call for her to make sure she was still there.

"Coming, coming," Bev said.

Finally, Bev saw a round, welcoming wooden door painted orange with green trim and small glass insets that glowed softly, complete with a knitted mat out front.

"Wipe your feet, please," the creature said as he opened the door for Bev.

She did as instructed, finding herself a good four feet shorter than the top of the doorframe. Inside, everything seemed larger than life—yet it was homey. A squishy couch covered in what appeared to be a hand-knitted quilt. In fact, most of the decorations seemed to have been knitted—the rug, the curtains, even the doilies on the tables. There was a large woven basket next to a giant chair, but Bev didn't see any knitting needles.

"Have a seat," he said. "Do you take honey in your tea?"

"Uh, sure," Bev said.

He disappeared into the kitchen, and Bev heard the distinct sound of a kettle over a fire. She peered around the open door, spotting a well-loved table and a hearth with a roaring fire.

She frowned. "Where does all the smoke go?" she asked. "From your kitchen?"

"Funnels out through a cave. Not trying to suffocate anyone." Using his long nails, he picked up a small tablespoon and dipped it into a canister, pouring the tea leaves into two porcelain mugs. In his hands, they looked normal-sized, but in Bev's... they would've been more like the large bowl she mixed her bread in.

"Where does all this come from?" Bev said. "I've never seen you in Pigsend."

"In the topside version of Pigsend," he said. "There's a thriving city just a few hours' walk from here. Lots of trading happening there. But the groundfolk don't mess with the topside folk much."

"I wasn't aware there was such a thing," Bev said. Though it *had* been mentioned by Eldred Nest a few times, Bev hadn't ever believed him.

"What you're aware of is quite limited then." He glanced in her direction. "My name's Merv, by the way. Do you have a name?"

"Bev." She tilted her head up to take in the rest of the house. There was a large crack in the ceiling that led to a partially collapsed wall. A few books poked out from the rubble and when Bev retrieved it, she found it three times the size of a normal book.

"That's the latest casualty," Merv said, his whiskers twitching unhappily. "But I've got cracks in my bedroom, my kitchen window has broken, and the back door sticks now. All these confounded earthquakes."

"And you aren't causing them?" Bev asked, turning to look at him.

"Heavens, no!" He bristled and his whiskers shook. "How in the world would I possibly do that?"

"I mean… If you're tunneling under the ground, then—"

"Our tunnels are *quite* sturdy, I assure you," he said, and Bev got the distinct impression that he, like the gnomes, was proud of his ability to manipulate the ground to the ignorance of those above. "And mine have been untouched since I dug them fifty years ago. At least, until *you* people started doing…*whatever* you're doing to cause all these earthquakes."

The kettle whistled, and within moments, Merv handed Bev an oversized porcelain teacup that she had to hold with both hands. She took a small whiff to prepare herself for what it might taste like and got notes of lavender and rosemary. Hesitantly, she took a sip.

"Delicious," she said with a smile.

"Thank you." He sat down in a well-worn, cushiony chair and put his feet up on the small ottoman—both covered in knitted blankets. And then he picked up an unfinished knitting project and used his long nails as knitting needles. Bev was amazed at the quickness with which he moved, and how gently the knots in the yarn came together.

"That's incredible," she said. "Have you made everything in this room?"

"Yes," he said with a proud smile. "It helps me think, you know, keeping the claws busy."

Bev smiled. "You know, there's a fiber arts competition at the annual Pigsend Harvest Festival. You should compete."

He bristled, and Bev could almost make out a blush. "Oh, I'm sure I wouldn't be in contention. These are silly little creations I make to pass the time." He nodded to an ajar door in the corner. "Have an entire closet full of nice blankets that are gathering dust."

Bev rose to inspect the closet. There were more blankets than she could count squeezed into every inch of the closet, all of them made from the most beautiful yarn Bev had ever seen.

"These are gorgeous," Bev said.

He tilted his head. "Would you like one?"

"Me? Oh, um—"

"I insist." He put down the project and waddled to join Bev near the closet. "What color would you like?"

"Surprise me," Bev said.

He plucked a nice purple and green one from the closet and handed it to her. It was softer than she'd anticipated, lacking the usual scratch of wool.

"Thank you," Bev said, running her hands along the blanket and glancing at Merv nervously—or rather, at his thick coat. "What…uh…kind of wool is it made from?"

"Tanddaes," he said. "I suppose the closest thing to a topsider creature is a sheep. One of my dear friends has a herd of them. They thrive in the darkness, like most creatures under here. They make the best blankets."

Bev had never heard of such a thing, but at least the fur wasn't his. She brought her new treasure back to the couch and sat down again. "Well, I suppose we should get to the business at hand, hm?"

Merv joined her, settling back into his chair and picking up his knitting project. "So you say you haven't a clue why these earthquakes are happening?"

"No," Bev said with a shake of her head. "The gnomes told me that someone was disturbing the river," Bev said, taking another sip of tea from the large cup. "So I went to check out the Pigsend Creek, and it was low. Found out who was draining it and yet…still we have earthquakes."

He took a sip, his whiskers moving out of the way to avoid falling in the hot liquid. "And they said creek?"

"River," Bev said.

"River and creek are not the same."

"I mean… there isn't another body of water around here," Bev said, gently balancing the cup in her lap as she felt rather dumb for ignoring her own instincts on the matter.

The mole chuckled. "Did they specify what *kind* of river was being disturbed?"

"Uh…there's only one kind, isn't there?"

"Oh-ho!" He put his paws on his stomach as he sat back on his haunches. "So much you know, topsider."

"I don't, actually," Bev said. "But if you'd like to enlighten me, I'd be appreciative."

"There are, in fact, many kinds of rivers. Rivers of air that move the grass—"

"So, wind."

"Semantics." He waved his hand. "And there are rivers of magic that flow all around us. Many of them can be found in the ground—which is most likely what your gnomes were digging for."

Bev sat up so suddenly she almost spilled her

tea. "That's what they were excavating, yeah! For the queen. So they *were* responsible."

"I'd be surprised," he said. "Gnomes aren't going to drain a resource just because—especially if it would cause damage to other areas."

Bev's excitement faded. They had mentioned the earthquakes were damaging their progress. "In any case, there wasn't magic to be found. At least the last time I spoke to them. The foreman told me they'd had a devil of a time trying to find it."

"Ah. That's interesting."

"Is it?" She picked up her tea to take another sip. "Why?"

"Well, gnomes are pretty good at sniffing out magic, eh? They wouldn't set up shop in a place where there wasn't magic recently. So that tells me someone *else* has been siphoning off the magic before they could get to it. And now the river of magic is completely gone." He nodded solemnly. "No magic, no stability in the earth. And thus…"

It did make sense. "How do we fix it?"

"You just have to find whoever's draining the magic and get them to stop." He smiled. "Easy, eh?"

"You're a man…um…mole of the earth," Bev said, carefully watching his expression to see if he was offended. "Who could do such a thing?"

"I wouldn't know," he said. "But if I were you, I'd follow the river. Magic is easily replenished. Give it an hour sometimes and it will bounce right back. So if it's still empty—to the point where the gnomes couldn't even get enough to do anything with—then someone is *actively* sucking it up."

"For what purpose?" Bev said. "Who could need that much magic?"

"Oh, lots of people need magic for lots of reasons." He chuckled. "The queen, I hear, is a big fan of it."

"She did just send a couple soldiers into town," Bev said, slowly. "And they have been awfully cagey about what they've been up to."

"I wouldn't think humans could handle that much magic," he said. "But what do I know, eh? I'm just a retired mole. I don't know much about the business of topsiders."

"But you know of the queen."

"Who doesn't?" He chuckled. "You think we were spared her nonsense?" His eyes grew a little sad. "Lots of good creatures had to hightail it out of town, you know?"

"Maybe they went even deeper underground," Bev offered.

He scoffed. "Don't be ridiculous. There is no *deeper*."

Bev didn't know enough to argue, so she just sipped her tea.

There was no way Bev could finish the gallon of tea and not float out of the mole's house, so she drank as much as was comfortable and took her leave. Merv insisted on walking her all the way back to the surface. He was nothing if not a hospitable host.

"Say Bev, what's your story, eh?" he asked. "There's something about you that seems…" He twitched his whiskers.

"Well, I don't really know," she said. "Showed up in town five years ago with amnesia. Who I was or what I did before is a mystery."

"Hm."

"But you're not the first person to say something like that," she said with a smile. "I usually just think it's because I have one of those faces, you know? Sort of person everyone met somewhere before."

"Oh, I can assure you, I've never met a person like you." He chuckled. "You've got the touch of someone who's seen magic before."

"Well, that's a new one!" Bev said with a chuckle as they reached the top of the tunnel. "These days, I'm a simple innkeeper. The only thing I want to touch is a nice potato or a scrubbing pail." She stepped out into the night sky; she hadn't realized she'd been down there for so long.

"This is where we part," Merv said.

"Thank you for the tea and for the blanket," Bev

said, squeezing the second item to her. "I appreciate the guidance, too. I promise, I'm working as fast as I can to find out what's really going on." She paused. "My inn is in danger of falling into one of those sinkholes, so I understand your concern."

"Then I wish you the best of luck," Merv said with a bow. "Now if you'll excuse me, I've got to get back to cleaning." He paused. "You know, I'd love it if you came to visit me again. Perhaps I'll leave the tunnel open for you."

Bev beamed. "That would be lovely. I'll be sure to visit as soon as these earthquakes calm down."

He bowed and turned to walk back into the darkness, and Bev waited until the sound of his shuffling feet had quieted before she headed back to Pigsend, her mind twisting with ideas and—

"Bev!" Ida called, running toward her. Vellora wasn't too far behind. "Bev, *where* have you been?"

"I was…" Bev gestured behind her, unsure how to explain what she'd just seen. "The gnomes are gone. I was—"

"It doesn't matter," Vellora said. "We've been looking all over for you. Shasta Brewer requested a town meeting. You're up to give an update on what's going on."

"I'm…what?" Bev blinked. "I don't have any."

"Tough, because the entire town is waiting for *you*!"

CHAPTER TWELVE

Bev would've rather skipped the town meeting, but Ida's firm grip on her left arm and Vellora's presence on her right kept her marching toward the town square.

"I don't have anything to share," Bev said. "I'm still trying to figure out what's going on."

"Do you have *any* clues?" Vellora asked. "Ida said you thought Trent had something to do with it."

"I did, but then we had another earthquake," Bev said. "But I just got a new tip that maybe the gnomes meant a *magical* river, and—"

"Whoa!" Ida barked, stopping her in her tracks.

"Are you *insane*? You can't go into the town meeting talking about magic!"

"Why not?"

"Because the queen's soldiers are in town," Vellora said, her face stony. "If they hear you mention that word, they'll drag you away." She tightened her grip on Bev's arm. "Promise me you won't even go there. *Promise me*."

"Oh, come now," Bev said with a small laugh. "The soldiers were perfectly fine talking with me about the gnomes."

"That's because the gnomes are so-called *approved* magic users, of which there are precious few," Ida said. "They do a service for the queen, so they're allowed to exist openly. But anyone else? Absolutely not." She licked her lips. "If they catch you with even a lick of magic, you could be arrested."

Bev frowned. Karolina and her team were rude, brusque, and didn't seem to think much of Pigsend, but she couldn't see them dragging people away for using a little magic.

"Bev, you don't... You don't remember what it was like before the war," Vellora said. "Right?"

She shook her head.

"This town was filled with all sorts of unique creatures," Ida said softly. "Everyone had a little bit of magic in their veins, it seemed. And they all just went about their business, harming no one. But when the Kingside lost, the soldiers came through town and sought out anyone who was openly using unapproved magic."

"That is, any magic the queen didn't think was useful to *her*," Vellora said.

Ida nodded. "It was a horrible time, Bev. Families torn apart. The queen was relentless in hunting down anything magical that didn't fit her needs, and now…" She glanced at her wife. "Now there's no magic left in any of us."

Or they've kept their powers quiet, Bev finished for her.

Ida certainly had something extra about that strength of hers. Others in town, too, seemed to be dancing on the precipice of openly using magic. Bev had never stopped to question why, but hearing it now…

"I understand your concern," she said. "But, look, if the magical river is being drained, and the gnomes couldn't find any in the area, wouldn't it be *beneficial* to the queen's mission if I figured out why?"

"They won't see it that way," Ida said softly. "They'll just see you associating with magic. That's all it takes."

"I'm sure that's not true. They've got to have some kind of discretion." But even Bev was losing her argument. Karolina didn't seem the sort of person to care about nuance. Perhaps the butchers had a point.

"Please trust us," Ida said. "We're not saying this to be contrary. We're trying to protect you."

"Fine," Bev said with a sigh. "No magic. But that's...that's the lead I have. And if the town's expecting an update, I don't have anything else."

"Then lie," Vellora said. "Or stall. Or say you don't have anything to report just yet."

"That'll go over worse than the magic stuff," Bev said.

"At least you'll still have your head," Ida said. "You can suffer through a few days of everyone being mad at you. But you can't recover from the soldiers taking you away."

Bev glanced between the nervous faces of her two dear friends and exhaled loudly. "Fine. I'll... figure something out, I guess."

~

The murmur of the crowd was audible even before the trio walked through the doors, but it immediately quieted. The eyes of everyone in the town were on Bev, as the butchers, having clearly done their duty of finding and delivering her to the town meeting, high-tailed it out of the line of fire.

Bev walked up the center of the hall—still holding Merv's hand-knitted blanket—like a bride to an ill-fated wedding. Ida and Vellora's warning swam in her mind, and she couldn't help but look out amongst the town and notice who seemed to be almost magical and who wasn't. It had never dawned on her why they all chose to keep their powers under wraps; she'd just thought it another quirk of living in a small town. Like someone having a grandfather who had invented something useful. A nice story to mention at parties, but nothing really impactful.

Then again, having the queen's soldiers—at least, those like Karolina and her compatriots—in town was quite rare. Perhaps once or twice in the five years Bev could remember, and the last group to visit didn't seem to have the…gravitas Karolina did. It could explain why the dangers of openly using magic hadn't come up in conversation.

But clearly, Bev was just spiraling, because she found herself at the front of the room without a clue what she was going to say to the waiting room of townsfolk. Mayor Hendry and Sheriff Rustin were sitting at their table, a third seat empty between them. Bev swallowed hard as she approached.

"Is it always this hostile?" Bev asked Hendry as she came to sit down.

The mayor shrugged. "Sometimes. You get used to it."

Bev doubted she would. "Hopefully, this is my

last town meeting in this position."

"I wouldn't count on it." Hendry rose and smiled as she lifted her hands. "Dear friends, thank you for coming to meet on such short notice. We're here to discuss an update to our last town meeting, the matter of the sinkholes."

A chorus of grumbles echoed from the crowd. Bev gazed out at her friends and neighbors and didn't see a friendly face in the bunch.

"I also wanted to share with you that Doc Howser has looked over our dear friend Stella Brewer and has declared she will make a full recovery." Hendry paused, and a few of the crowd looked placated, but not many. "Well, Bev, I turn the floor over to you." As she sat down, the mayor muttered under her breath, "I tried to warm them up for you."

Bev rose slowly, spotting Trent Scrawl in the back of the room. He looked nervous—and while he would have made an easy scapegoat, she didn't think it was fair to blame him for something he didn't have anything to do with.

"I went to visit the gnome nest outside town," Bev began slowly. "The foreman of the group informed me that the reason for the sinkholes was due to a disruption in the river. I know you've all noticed that it's been...low lately."

"Practically dried up!" Etheldra barked from the

front row.

"Couldn't even get water from our pumps," Herman Monday cried, earning a smile from Trent.

Bev wrenched her gaze away from them. "And thankfully, we've had a nice deluge to refill the coffers. I had hoped that would solve the problem, but it seems—"

"Seems those gnomes lied to you," Bardoff called.

"Yeah, they're doing it, and they don't want to get caught!"

"We should show them what's what!"

"Go out there ourselves and demand answers!"

"Before you break out your pitchforks," Hendry said, her voice ringing out clear and beautifully over the chaos. "I will remind you that the gnomes are under the queen's protection. And I will also remind you that there are five very capable soldiers in town who could mete justice out to anyone who interferes with their business."

The threat of the queen quieted the room but didn't soothe their angry faces.

"I will say," Bev began after another pause, "that it seemed to me the gnomes were as troubled by the earthquakes as we are. They had to rebuild their scaffolding every time one occurred. They also… insisted that they couldn't be the ones who were causing the problems because they're so far out of town." The angry grumbling began again. "And it appears they've been gone for at least two days."

That seemed to get the attention of the crowd.

"Is it possible they got what they wanted and left?" Hendry asked, almost intimating the word *magic*. "And we're left with the aftermath?"

"That all depends on if you think the queen would send her people to a town she controls in order to cause chaos," Bev replied, choosing her words carefully.

Hendry seemed to consider them before clearing her throat. "Well, if we have no more earthquakes, perhaps the problem will resolve itself."

Bev sensed that the mayor was giving her an out, and she nodded. "We can only hope."

"But in case it doesn't," Hendry said, immediately turning back to the crowd, "does anyone have any ideas to share with Bev?"

~

"Well, that was an extremely productive evening," Vellora said as she, Ida, and Bev walked back to their houses. "You know, I love to hear how much Herman Monday and Trent Scrawl hate each other."

"Indeed," Bev said with a soft smile. "But hey, at least it's only nine in the evening instead of two. Perhaps the shortest town meeting in the history of Pigsend."

"We'll mark it down in the town annals," Vellora said.

"Speaking of time, where the heck were you all afternoon, Bev? Those soldiers came looking for you to pay you for another night. It's a good thing the chicken Vellora was dressing was already dead." She glanced at the blanket Bev still clung to like a child's lovey. "And where the heck did you get that blanket?"

"If I tell you, promise you won't think I'm completely mad?" Bev said.

"Never." Ida squeezed her arm. "I always think you're a little bit mad."

"Then come on in for a cuppa," Bev said. "Because you're going to need one."

The three women sat around one of the tables in the front room, and Bev added a little whiskey to all three of their teas. As she sat on one of the stools, she told Ida and Vellora about Merv appearing near where the gnomes had been, about how he'd invited her down into his cave and given her tea and a knitted blanket as they talked about the earthquakes. As predicted, both women stared slack-jawed at Bev until she finished.

"That's…" Ida took a long sip of tea. "You were right to question your sanity."

"And what did he say that blanket is made of?" Ida asked, pulling it over to her and taking a long sniff. "Doesn't smell like a wild animal."

"I can't even remember the name," Bev said with a chuckle. "But apparently, they're bred like sheep in this underground community he told me about."

Vellora ran her fingers along the fabric. "You should get more. A blanket for every room in the inn. You said he had a closet full of them, right?"

"I wouldn't mind getting one for our bed," Ida said, pulling the blanket around herself. "This is cozy."

"I'm not sure if I'll ever see him again," Bev said with a chuckle. "He seemed pretty happy to hide away in the underground. Seemed to be a whole thing for him to make his way to the topside, as he called it."

"Do you think you can trust him?" Vellora asked. "You said the ground shook when he popped up, right?"

She nodded. "But it wasn't the same. It was much less violent." She put down her teacup. "You know, I like to think of myself as a good judge of character. Got gut feelings about people. Maybe it's because I don't remember much about my past life, or maybe it's because I had some kind of sense before but..."

"Bev?"

"I don't think the gnomes *or* Merv are the cause

of the sinkholes," Bev said, looking up at them. "Because if the gnomes were, why would they tell me about the river?"

"To be fair, they were cagey about it," Ida said. "They said river—"

"And they left," Vellora said.

"Merv said magic replenishes itself quickly, so even if they were responsible, the problem should have resolved once they stopped," Bev said. "Clearly, whoever is draining the magical river, they're still doing it."

"Bet you it's those soldiers," Vellora said, keeping her voice low as she glanced toward the front door of the kitchen. "Wouldn't put it past them."

"And they're not completely off the hook, either," Bev said with a nod. She *had* seen one of them out there in the forest near Trent's farm. "But as you two made abundantly clear to me today, messing with them isn't the best course of action. If I'm to accuse them of something, I'd better have all my facts together."

The butchers nodded. "So what do you do now?" Vellora asked.

"If the magical river is what's being drained, maybe the first step is finding the river itself."

"How the heck do you do that?" Ida asked.

Bev grew quiet, and soon the only sound was

the ticking clock. "I haven't the foggiest. No one around here knows anything about magic, right?"

"Thanks to the queen, no," Vellora said. "And if they did, they wouldn't advertise it."

"I bet you could find something in the library," Ida said thoughtfully. "There's probably maps and almanacs from decades past—before the war. There has to be at least a mention of the magical river there."

Bev nodded. "That's a good idea."

"But I wouldn't let the librarian know you're looking for it," Vellora said. "No telling who can be trusted."

"Except us, of course," Ida added with a bright smile. "You know we're always on your side."

Bev smiled at the couple. "And it's appreciated. I don't know why this thing came to me, but I'm intent on seeing it through until the very end."

Ida reached across the table to take Bev's hand. "Just please, be careful. You walking down into mole holes and skulking around Trent's farmland at night... You could scare the wrong person, you know? Or worse, end up afoul of your lovely tenants before you have the facts."

"And even if you have the facts," Vellora said, "there's no telling if you'll be able to *do* anything about it, if the queen's soldiers are the responsible party."

Bev had already considered that as well. "We'll cross that bridge when we come to it. But for now, more sneaking around seems to be the name of the game for me." She sighed and glanced at the unopened bags of flour in the corner. "One day, perhaps, I'll get back to the business of being an innkeeper."

CHAPTER THIRTEEN

Bev awoke the next morning and sped through her chores. She was running low on hay for the horses, and the kitchen wasn't nearly as clean as Wim McKee would've expected, but she wanted to get down to business. She hadn't the foggiest idea how she was going to find a book on magic, let alone find it without Max the librarian noticing. A clever spy, she certainly was not.

Once the clock struck ten, she left the inn and walked toward the library. She paced around the town square, stopping to examine the sinkhole there and trying to appear as if she wasn't searching for the librarian.

Max didn't seem to be on his stool, but that didn't mean he wasn't around. She winced as the bell jingled above her head and held her breath. But she didn't hear the librarian, nor did he call out in greeting, so she silently closed the door behind her.

She crossed the room in three steps and scanned the spines of the books just behind his counter. Almanacs from years ago. Not useful. So she walked to the shelf just behind it, finding more almanacs. Her pulse spiking, she crossed the room and found mundane books on gardening, pottery, and other homemaking skills.

"Bev! I didn't hear you come in!"

She went stick straight as Max emerged from the back office with a smile.

"Hey, Max," she said, hoping she didn't sound guilty. "Good to see you again."

"And you, as well. Are you here to return that encyclopedia? No need for you to hang onto it if the gnomes are gone."

"Uh." Bev had completely forgotten about it. "I'll bring it to you soon. I'm actually here in search of something…else." She turned to the stacks, needing to buy some time. "Allen Mackey asked me to find some recipe books," she said, thinking quickly. "Would you have any around?"

"You know, I just might." He held up one finger with a smile. "Give me a minute to search."

Once he was gone, Bev exhaled and briskly walked through the stacks. She found one or two shelves of nonfiction, but even that wasn't what she was looking for. Then, as she crossed the center aisle, she paused and stared at the back of the library where a half-open door led to Max's office.

Magic was a taboo subject, so if one *were* looking for a book about said subject, perhaps it wouldn't be out in the main stacks but back in the librarian's office under lock and key. Slowly, she began to walk toward the door when Max appeared out of nowhere.

"There you are!" he announced cheerfully. "I found a couple options for you. This one is more about cooking, so I don't think Mr. Mackey will be able to use it, but these two are about baking." He brightened. "I tell you, I'm looking forward to those scrumptious muffins once again. It's been ages since he's made a good batch!"

"Agreed," Bev said with a nervous smile as she took the two books on baking.

"Is there anything else I can do for you?" he asked, tilting his head.

"Nope." Bev pulled the books to her. "That'll be all for now!"

She didn't want to admit defeat, but if she kept asking for more books on different subjects, Max would get confused. The only thing to do was to watch the library to see if he left for lunch, but that would require her to be away from the inn for longer than she'd like. She already needed to get carrots and hay, and the time was ticking closer to prep for dinner.

This was going to have to be another after-hours adventure. Bev sure was getting tired of those.

~

Bev managed to get hay for the horses, but carrots were harder to come by, so she had to go without. Dinner was another story, with a meager number of potatoes to go with the chicken. Complaints were heard from the usual crowd of diners, including Etheldra, who seemed convinced that Bev was being lazy for not making the confounded rosemary bread.

"Any news on the sinkholes?" Earl asked as he handed Bev his empty plate.

"Working on it," she said with a tense smile. "I hope."

"Maybe you should pick up the pace, eh?" he said, a little rudely as he walked out the back door.

Might be able to spend more time on it if I wasn't feeding you lot every night, she thought grumpily.

But tending to the inn was the only thing normal about her life these days, and she would miss it terribly if she skipped a day.

Once the patrons were gone, Bev quickly

cleaned up and swiped her cloak from the pin near the back door since it was a bit chilly—not to mention it helped with the whole "sneaking around" vibe that she was apparently into these days. Then she stuffed her hands in her pockets and headed out into the silent streets.

The walk to the library was even longer than the nighttime walk to Trent's house. Every shadow seemed to accuse her of heresy, of breaking the public trust. She chewed her lip and whispered to herself that this was, in fact, the *safest* option for her.

The building loomed large in front of her, bathed in shadow from the moonless night. The first problem, of course, was how to get inside. She wasn't going to break any windows, and she knew nothing about picking locks. She held her breath and walked up to the front door. How trusting was the old librarian?

She exhaled softly as the knob turned under her hand.

"Very trusting, indeed," she muttered. Then again, why would Max need to lock his door? It wasn't as if there was an abundance of thieves and trespassers in Pigsend.

Except, obviously, for Bev.

Quickly, she let herself inside, wincing at the sound of the bell. She waited a breath to see if Max, who she assumed lived upstairs, had heard. After a tense few moments, she relaxed and kept walking toward the back office.

It seemed every step she took was on a creaky floorboard, echoing in the silence as loudly as a braying donkey. Finally, she reached Max's office and turned the knob, saying a silent prayer of thanks when it, too, turned and allowed her entry.

The librarian's office was as one would expect— crammed with books, papers, and a cold mug of tea on a well-worn stone coaster. Curiosity got her for a moment, and she peered down to see what he was working on. The page was open to this week, and there was an accounting of the town's activities, including the earthquakes, Stella's near-death experience, and Bev's short town meeting. She flipped the pages back, keeping her finger on the current week, and found an accounting of harvest totals from each farmer. It amazed her that Pigsend kept records like that, but there was a purpose, perhaps, to everything.

She set the book back the way she'd found it and turned to gaze at the stacks of books. Some looked to be returned library books, and others had papers jutting out between the leaves. She stood on her toes and reached for the book on top of the stack.

But when she pulled it down, the stack began to teeter.

"Oh no," Bev whispered. "No, no—"

She frantically pushed the books backward, but that was the wrong move, too, and they toppled to the ground in a crash that seemed so loud, Bev wouldn't have been surprised if it had woken everyone in town. Panicked, she wavered between running out the door and picking up her mess, but before she could make a decision, footsteps echoed on the creaky floorboard.

"Bev?" Max stood in the center of the library, holding his lantern aloft. "What in the world are you doing here at this hour? And in my office?"

Bev opened and closed her mouth, running through plausible reasons that didn't involve the truth. But after a few moments of stunned silence, she decided it was better to come clean with Max than have him turn her into Rustin for trespassing.

"Can you keep a secret?" Bev asked, slowly. "Specifically from…people who might not want me investigating what I'm investigating?"

"Of course, but—"

"I think the reason we're having the earthquakes is because someone's disrupted the natural flow of magic in town," she said. "And I need to find out where that flow actually is before I can figure out who's disrupting it."

The old librarian's face lit up with shock. "I see."

Bev licked her lips. "I promise, I didn't mean to

make such a mess. And I obviously didn't want to come in after hours." She paused. "But I couldn't just come out with what I was doing because—"

"Of those soldiers." He nodded again and actually seemed a bit less put-out. "I can see why you thought it better to sneak around than come to me. But you know, Bev, I'm the keeper of the town's secrets—that includes those held by her citizens."

She exhaled and smiled. "I appreciate that."

"However, I'm not going to be much help," he said, picking up one of the books on the floor and putting it back in the stack. "Magic and magical arts have all been eradicated from the library. I don't know if you'll find anything in here to help you."

"I was hoping maybe one of the older maps of the town might show something," Bev said. "It's a long shot, but—"

"I see." He put his finger to his chin. "Give me a moment."

He disappeared, but not into his office. Instead, he walked over to the shelves holding old, yellowed scrolls. He ran his finger along each until he found the one he was looking for and brought it over to Bev, rolling it out onto the table.

"This is a map from twenty years ago—before the war," he said. "When magic was much more prevalent in these parts."

Bev nodded as she peered down. Most

everything was the same as today, including the houses, the creek, even the Weary Dragon Inn. To her untrained eye, there wasn't anything that denoted a magical river, and she watched the old librarian's face for any sign that he saw something she didn't.

"No," he said. "I'm not sure how I could help you find it."

"You gave me the book on magical creatures," Bev said. "Maybe there's a book on… I don't know. Magic finding? Magic uses? Ways to excavate a magical river?"

He shook his head slowly. "None come to mind, I'm afraid. But…" He gestured to a small bookcase that had locked glass doors. "You're welcome to search what I have in the so-called restricted section. But take care that you aren't seen, and whatever you find…keep to yourself. I would be in trouble if those soldiers even knew I kept such things." He adjusted his nightshirt. "They came through right after the war—the librarians from the Queen's Capital. Sorted through our entire collection and took what they assumed was 'inappropriate' reading material." He sighed sadly. "I don't think I've ever cried as hard as when I saw the bonfire."

Bev knelt beside him as he unlocked the bookshelf, sensing his pain. "How did you get these, then?"

"Oh, you know, here and there. Folks had them in their houses, or they were family heirlooms nobody wanted to keep anymore after the purge. Some perhaps…perhaps intentionally kept them hidden." He brightened. "I hope you find what you're looking for in here. If you don't mind, I'm quite tired after the day, and I'd like to go back to bed."

"Please," Bev said with a kind smile. "I'll be sure to clean up before I leave."

When the clock struck two in the morning, Bev was still carefully leafing through the books in the glass bookcase. They perhaps didn't need such a delicate touch, but knowing they were most likely the last of their kind in town, she wanted to preserve as much as possible.

But after perusing three or four different books, she was starting to grow weary. The magic described in this book was benign—charms for growing crops, strengthening masonry mortar, that sort of thing. The others had been similar, with one being a history of notable magic makers that seemed to stop about five hundred years before.

She let out a yawn, rubbing her eyes and deciding whether she wanted to try again tomorrow. But the clock was ticking—both literally and figuratively. There would be another earthquake, and the next victim might not be as lucky as Stella Brewer.

With that bit of worry, Bev plucked another book from the stack. It was a primer on all things farming, which was an odd thing to have stuck in the prohibited section, but Bev trusted that Max hadn't made a mistake.

Then, just as her eyes were about to close, she hit pay dirt.

Magical Rivers

As one scours the land in search of good sun, soil, and water, it is also important to consider the presence of a nearby magical river. Now, while most humans can't wield magic without a little help, building a farm in close proximity to a magical river will aid in the robustness, variety, and health of crops. A magical river might also ensure long life and good vitality for the farmer, as well.

She leaned in, pulling the lantern closer so she could see better.

FINDING A MAGICAL RIVER

The best way to find a good magical river source is to enlist the help of a magical sniffer, like a werehound or a laelaps. If no such creature is available for hire, then a regular human can construct a magical dowsing rod in a pinch, though the effects may vary.

On the next page, there was a drawing of a farmer holding a Y-shaped stick over the ground. It had small arrows pointing to the left, showing that the magic could be found that way. Bev held her breath as she kept reading.

DOWSING RODS

When making a magical dowsing rod, it's best to source from the tree of a willow, witch hazel, or peach. Simply pluck the branch off and hold as illustrated.

> Then, feel for the sensation of tugging in the stick. When the stick points down, you can be assured that a large thread of magic runs underground.

Bev sat back, chewing her lip. That seemed easy enough, though she didn't really know much about trees or where to find them. But she knew a few people who might.

Silently, she closed the book and put it and the others back into the shelves the way she'd found them. Then she slipped the small, silver key into the lock, ensuring it was tight before placing the key back in Max's desk in the front before slipping out the front door and closing it tightly behind her. The night air was fresh against her hot cheeks, and even though she was *very* tired, she felt a new sense of purpose.

Next step: find a magical dowsing rod.

CHAPTER FOURTEEN

The late nights were starting to catch up to Bev, as she slept through her usual wakeup time of sunrise. Sin seemed furious that her breakfast was an hour or two delayed, as did the guest horses, who'd become accustomed to the schedule Bev usually held fast to.

"So very sorry, Your Majesties," Bev said with a yawn as she grabbed her rake to muck their stalls. "Duty calls, you know."

Though she would've rather taken a long nap after her morning chores, instead, she found herself out and about again, walking down the street toward the person who knew more about plants than anyone else in town—Vicky Hamblin. One of the downfalls of having lost her entire memory was that things she perhaps should've known—like identifying different types of trees—were foreign to her. Unless it had a growing fruit or vegetable on it, Bev was hopelessly lost.

Vicky, however, seemed to have a connection with all things green—not just the food the farmers grew, but the flowers, grasses, trees, even the thorny sticker bushes that drove everyone mad. Given enough time, Vicky would explain exactly how a particular plant, no matter how much of a nuisance, was essential to the overall health of the world.

The young lady was hard at work in Apolinary's seamstress shop, sitting in a cushiony chair with a purple skirt splayed across her lap as she embroidered a flower pattern. Apolinary was nowhere to be seen, which suited Bev just fine. Vicky was the only one she needed to speak with, and it would be easier if there wasn't an audience.

Bev pushed open the door and the small bell above her tinkled. Vicky looked up, eager to greet whoever had walked inside until she registered Bev —then she scowled.

"Oh. It's you."

Bev forced a smile. "How's Stella feeling?"

"Doc Howser said she just needs to rest for a few days," Vicky said, her words tight and clipped. "But otherwise, she's all right. The twins are staying with me for the moment."

"Above the shop?" Bev asked with a frown. "Don't you just have the one room?"

She speared the skirt with her needle as if it had personally wronged her. "It's cramped, but it's fine. Earl says he should be able to get their house rebuilt in a few weeks."

"I have a spare bedroom at the inn," Bev said. "I'd be happy to—"

"No." Vicky shook her head firmly. "No, I don't think they want to risk falling into another sinkhole."

"Ah, well, yeah. That's…" Bev cleared her throat. Something told her that wasn't the *only* reason. "That's a good idea."

"Was that all you wanted? To check on Stella?" From her tone it was clear she wanted this conversation to end as quickly as possible.

Bev almost hated to ask her, but no one was better suited to answer the question. "No, actually. Do we have any willow trees in town? Or witch hazel? Peach, even?"

She looked up, narrowing her gaze at Bev. "Why?"

"Just curious." Bev put her hands behind her back.

"Does this have anything to do with the

sinkholes?" Vicky asked. "Because it seems to me *that* should be your only focus at the moment."

"I promise you, it does." She hoped she wouldn't have to explain further. Vicky didn't seem to be too loyal to the queen, but she was mad enough at Bev that she might let the magical stuff slip to the soldiers out of spite. "Before the gnomes left, they shared with me a way I might be able to... uh...locate the disturbances. I need a branch from one of those trees."

"Are you sure they haven't just sent you on a wild goose chase?"

"They might have, indeed," Bev said. "But right now, it's the only thread I've got to pull on, so to speak. So I'm pulling until it stops unraveling."

Vicky made a noise and didn't answer.

"Vicky, I know you're angry with me. But the sooner I find these trees, the sooner I can put a pin in this and...try something else." Bev leaned on the counter and put on her best smile. "Please? I really don't know who else to turn to."

Vicky sighed and put down the project. "Fine. You won't find any peaches in town. The closest orchard is perhaps fifty miles to the south of here. Witch hazel is a bit tricky. If you can get by with a willow tree, Rosie Kelooke has a very mature one in her front yard." She pointedly ran her finger along her stitching. "Doc Howser used a great deal of bark to help Stella with the pain. It's good for that, you know."

"I'm glad to hear it," Bev said. "So Rosie's got the best one? I'll have to pay her a visit."

Vicky nodded. "Be warned: She won't give up pieces of it for free. I hear Doc had to make her a few tinctures for her gout in order to get some. And for you, well…" She exhaled stiffly. "Rosie blames you for destroying her prized oven, so you're going to have to really beg for it, I'd wager."

Bev winced. Another enemy made in town through no fault of her own. "And there's…no one else in town who might have a willow tree?"

Vicky shook her head, digging her needle into the skirt.

"Well, maybe I should whip up that rosemary bread I've been promising people," Bev said with a sigh. "Thanks for the tip, Vicky."

She made a dismissive noise, as if telling Bev to leave.

Bev was halfway out the door, before she stopped and turned back to ask, "Say, have you and Allen made up yet? I haven't seen him around lately, and I was wondering…if…"

Vicky looked up, and for a split second, Bev was sure the girl was going to throw her out. Instead, she burst into tears, burying her face in the skirt.

"Oh, sweetheart, I'm sorry," Bev said, running

over. "I shouldn't have asked."

"No, no, I just...I haven't been able to talk about it with anyone," she said, wiping her eyes with the skirt Bev was sure didn't belong to her. "Allen's just been so distant lately. I don't know what's going on with him. He's not been himself for days now. He won't talk to me. Slammed the door in my face when I tried to bring him something to eat this morning."

Bev came closer to her, offering a sad smile. "Do you think maybe...maybe he's just fallen out of love with you? People fall in and out of love all the time."

She shook her head furiously. "No, Bev. We were... It's like he changed overnight. I caught him sneaking into the dark forest outside town and he got... Bev, he was so mad. I was scared he'd do something to hurt me!" She sniffed loudly. "Just last week, we were talking about taking a trip to Middleburg and now he's..."

Bev patted her knee. "I saw him going into the dark forest last week, too. Do you know what he might be doing?"

"Only terrible things live there," she said. "Whatever he's got himself into has rooted itself into his being, changed his personality. Made him... made him a different man than the one I fell in love with."

"I'm sure he'll come around," Bev said,

squeezing her hand. "I'll keep an eye out for him, and if I see him, I'll knock some sense into him. No telling what he might be mixed up with that forest."

She nodded. "T-thank you. I'm s-sorry I was snappy earlier. Just with all these sinkholes and now Allen acting strangely, I haven't slept in d-days. I'm s-so on edge. F-f-feel like the world is going to collapse any minute now."

"No apologies needed," Bev said. "Why don't you whip yourself up some calming draught and take a break from work, hm? You look like…" The skirt was covered in tears and perhaps a little snot. "You look like you could use it."

She nodded and wiped her nose on the skirt again. "Thanks, Bev. I think I'll do that." She offered Bev a small smile. "And good luck. I hope you find what you're looking for."

～

Bev chewed on this new tidbit of information about Allen, unsure when or how she'd be able to act on it. Vicky would've known better than Bev about Allen's mood change; he'd been a bit shifty with Bev since they'd met. She did worry about the kid, of course, but until she solved the bigger problem, he'd have to sort through his own mess.

Since retiring from the seamstress shop, Rosie had thrown herself into all manner of activities. Her front yard had been transformed into a lush, beautiful garden (though, of course with the drought, everything was a bit brown and withered). Tall trees swayed in front of her quaint house, their trunks surrounded by white rocks carefully laid in a perfect circle. The path to the house was gravel, flanked on either side by raised planter boxes. On one, trellises held empty berry vines. The other was a cascade of tomatoes, marigolds, and root vegetables.

Bev carefully undid the latch on the gate and let herself inside, listening for the sounds of chicken squawks. Rosie's chickens were legendary in town—they were called krooke chickens, with large puffs atop their feathered heads and a mean streak a mile wide. Based on the sound of clucking, they were corralled in the back of the house, so Bev took her time walking up the gravel path to the front door.

"Rosie?" Bev called, walking up the steps. "Are you around?"

The two trees in the yard were close to the house, providing shade from the sun. One of them had branches that swept the ground, almost looking like the leaves were water cascading down a waterfall—the willow, most likely. The other was a bushy, rounded tree that Bev was fairly sure was a maple.

Rosie wasn't around; Bev *could* have snuck under the willow and snapped off a branch. But knowing Rosie, it was probably better to ask for permission.

"Rosie, are you home?"

The pebbles on the ground began to shake, and for a brief moment, Bev feared there might be another earthquake coming. Instead, a barrage of chickens appeared from around the corner. Perhaps fifty of them—some white, some brown, some speckled different colors, all with that telltale puff atop their head—practically flew into the front garden, clucking and squawking and pecking at everything they could get their beaks on—including Bev's shoes and her pant legs.

"Oi! Cut it out!" she said, gently pushing the birds away. "Rosie? Hello? Are you here?"

The chickens were undaunted, surrounding her quickly. She tried to move onto the front steps, but the chickens followed to continue pecking, squawking, and clawing at Bev. She glanced around and gently kicked one that was particularly aggressive down the stairs, but another took its place.

"I'll thank you not to hurt my birds." Rosie had opened her living room window and was staring out at Bev with a decidedly unfriendly expression. "What do you want?"

"Oh, well—" Bev winced as the chickens came for her again. "Maybe call off the chickens, and we can talk?"

"I'll call off the chickens when you tell me what

you want."

Bev winced as a pointed beak found the underside of her knee and another her shin. "I wanted—*ouch!*—to see if I could—*eek!*—borrow a bit of willow from you. A—*jeez!*—branch, really."

"Why would I let you have that?" she said. "Are you going to use it to whack the gnomes so they'll quit destroying our town?"

Bev forced a smile onto her face. "Remember, I said at the town meeting that they'd moved on."

"And left our town to deal with the aftermath of their destruction," she said. "Clearly, whatever they extracted from the soil was needed for the stability of the ground."

"That's not—*yeouch*—what—*goodness!*—happened," Bev said.

"Harrumph. Lying little monsters," Rosie said. "I suppose they didn't tell you where they were going, hm? Just came here and left our town in shambles! My poor oven." She put her hand to her heart. "Ten years I saved up to have Jane and Earl build that for me. It was meticulously designed, beautifully crafted. And now it's a pile of junk at the bottom of a hole."

Bev shook her head. "It was absolutely a tragedy, but—"

"And the poor Brewer girls! You know, they may never sleep again!" She put her hands on her hips, leaning toward Bev with an accusatory look on her face. "You should've just let us march down there and drag their little butts into town to answer for their crimes."

"And as the mayor—*goodness me!*—said last night," Bev cried, pushing three demonic chickens off. "They're protected. You're—*ow!*—a fan of the queen. Surely, you understand."

But Rosie's opinion of Queen Meandra seemed to have soured, along with her opinion of Bev.

"Look," Bev was finally close enough to Rosie that the chickens left her alone. She exhaled as she wiped her forehead. "I understand you have doubts. But for me to get to the bottom of what *is* happening, I need to borrow a willow branch."

"What do you need it for?" she asked.

"Uh…" What was a plausible reason for needing a willow branch? "Because it can help…summon the gnomes back." It was a stretch that Rosie would believe such a thing, and it was veering on a magical solution, but it was the only thing Bev could come up with on the spot.

She held her breath as the old woman considered her request. "Make me a loaf of that rosemary bread and you've got a deal."

Bev nodded. "I've got a list of folks to make it for, and you're on it."

"It's the one to your left," she said, nodding to

the weeping tree. "And if you need some for pain, you're better off chewing it than making tea. No matter what that goof Vicky Hamblin might think."

Bev turned to the tree with the branches that reached toward the ground. She ducked under the leaves, touching each of the branches until she saw one with two points like the book had instructed. Then she snapped it off and reappeared on the other side.

"Um, thanks!"

"I'll be expecting that rosemary bread within the next day or so," Rosie called as Bev let herself out of the gate, eager to get away from the retired seamstress and her killer chickens.

Chapter Fifteen

With her precious dowsing rod in hand, Bev returned to the inn to sit at the front desk for a few hours to nurse her wounds and wait for evening. It was a welcome respite from all the sneaking around, and Bev considered how fortunate she'd been that no one had come by looking for a place to sleep during her adventures. Still, she felt like she'd been neglecting her beloved inn, even though all her efforts had been to save it from falling into a sinkhole.

The willow branch sat pressed against her leg. Not as if anyone would look twice at her for carrying around a stick, but she didn't want to advertise what she was doing, in case the queen's soldiers knew something about dowsing rods. Said soldiers had come down right as Bev had settled into her chair and plunked another five gold coins down on the desk.

"Another night," Bev said with a smile. "Will you be needing dinner?"

"No." Karolina turned and walked toward the back door. "Will you be fixing the hole in the front of the inn any time soon?"

Bev nodded weakly. "Hopefully within the next week."

"Well, see that you do. It's very cumbersome to come and go through the servant's quarters."

Servant's…? "You mean the kitchen?" Bev asked with a bit of a smile.

"Same thing." She disappeared through the door without another word.

Bev perhaps should've asked if they wanted laundry done again or their sheets changed, but if she were being honest, she didn't have time—and she didn't think they'd want her in their business anyway. Wim McKee's voice echoed in her ear about being a hospitable host, and she dismissed it.

"Can't be a host if we don't have an inn, Wim," she muttered.

Dinner was approaching soon, and Bev was scraping the bottom of the barrel—literally—for veggies to add to her chicken pot pie. Tomorrow, without fail, she would have to visit the farmers again and hope all the rain had brought their crops back to life. Today, she got extra chicken from the butchers to round out stew and made a crust of lard, water, and a little leavening. Then she popped the large iron pot into the stone oven.

The usual crowd was a little thinner tonight, with only Earl and Bardoff showing up to have a meal. They said little to Bev, and she got the distinct impression they were also cross with her—though not cross enough to skip out on a meal.

With a full belly, at least Earl tipped his cap and wished Bev a good night as they exited through the back door. She waved, and once they were gone, cleaned up quickly, then plucked the dowsing rod from behind the counter and headed outside.

She wasn't quite sure where to start, but logic told her that if the sinkholes appeared due to lack of magic in the river, then the river must've run at least near the holes. Perhaps if she took the dowsing rod near the sinkholes, she might pick up on a faint thread of magic.

It was a shot in the dark, to be sure—what Bev knew about magic couldn't fill a thimble—but it was the best she could do under the circumstances, and she certainly didn't feel like an idiot walking with a stick in hand hoping to feel the tug of magic.

Nor did she feel stupid pointing said stick at the center of the sinkhole and waiting.

Something tugged.

It was faint. But the longer she stood there, the more she felt it. Tugging, pulling, whatever, like a weak hand had taken the tip and was guiding it in a direction. She kept a loose grip on the ends, stumbling forward as the dowsing rod led her down the street. She was, yet again, grateful for the cover of night because she didn't want to know what people would think if they saw her wandering like this.

She was so focused on the tugging feeling and making sure she was following it that she didn't even notice it had led her into the center of town, right to where the second sinkhole had taken the Pigsend fountain.

"Well, I'll be," Bev said with a shake of her head and a smile. Maybe there was something to this after all.

She kept walking, the dowsing rod taking her to the right this time. Based on the path, she had a hunch it would lead to Rosie Kelooke's backyard. The old woman was inside on her floral-covered couch, reading a book by candlelight. Bev hurried along, hoping she wouldn't be seen—either by the old woman or her murder chickens.

The trail very obviously led into her backyard,

but the sound of Rosie's chickens clucking sleepily kept Bev from hopping the fence. Instead, she hung the dowsing rod over it and walked until she felt the tug away from Rosie's house. It seemed to want to double back, except taking the next road over. Bev didn't know anything about magical rivers, so maybe they were windy and unwieldy. She passed back through the center of town, near to the fountain, then continued along the path—this time headed for the Brewers' house. Beyond that, the trail led her out of town, past the original sinkhole, and toward…

Toward the dark forest.

She groaned. She didn't want to go into the dark forest *at all*. Not in the dark, and most certainly not *alone*.

"Bev?"

She jumped as Sheriff Rustin came trotting up next to her holding a lantern.

"Sherriff, hi," Bev said, clearing her throat as she hid the dowsing rod behind her back. "What can I do for you?"

"What are you doing out so late at night?" he asked. "And looking at the forest. Don't tell me you're going in there! Bad enough in the daytime, but at night…"

"No, of course not," Bev said with a half-smile. "Just stretching my legs in the night air."

"Whatcha got behind your back?" he asked, peering around. "Is that…"

Bev held her breath.

"A fishing pole?"

She chuckled. "No. It's not. Just…some willow branch from Rosie's yard. Helps with the aches and pains, you know? Grabbed a branch on my way home to make some tea once I get back to the inn."

"Oh, well, I hope you asked Ms. Rosie if you could have some. I hear she's fit to be tied with you," Rustin said, rubbing his nose. "I think most of the folks in town are."

Bev forced a tense smile. "What about you? Any luck finding the cause for the sinkholes?"

"Not at all," he said. "I tell ya, I don't even know the first place to look. Who does one talk to about this sort of stuff?" He barked a laugh as he bent over. "Hello? Mr. Ground? Can you tell me why you're shaking and crumbling all over the place?" He put his hands on his belly and chuckled. "To be honest, Bev, I've been busy tending to the queen's soldiers, and I haven't had a moment to even think about anything else."

"Oh?" Bev frowned. "They still have you running all over town?"

He nodded. "They tell me where to be and to keep the townsfolk out of their way. That's all they really want from me. Stand around and make sure nobody gets near them." He rubbed the back of his neck. "If you ask me, I say they just don't want to associate with us farm folk. All they're doing is digging in the dirt."

"Digging in the dirt?" Bev said. "Are they looking for something? Do they seem to be pulling anything out of the ground?"

"Whatever they're doing, they don't let me see," he said. "But I do get the distinct impression that whatever they're looking for, they haven't found. Every day, they get meaner and meaner, and I just…" He sighed, forlornly. "You know, I'd just like a thank-you every once in a while for all my help."

Bev put a hand on his shoulder. "Thank you, Rustin, for all the work you do. The town is immeasurably safer thanks to your efforts."

He brightened. "Thanks, Bev. But be warned, the soldiers are doing their…whatever it is they're doing over this way. So you might want to steer clear tonight."

She nodded. "I was going to head back to the inn anyway. Hope they don't keep you out too late!"

~

Bev didn't head back to the inn because she was tired, or even because she wanted to avoid the soldiers. No, the thought of venturing into the dark forest alone and after dark was about as appetizing as facing Rosie's chickens again. But Rustin's appearance, plus the dowsing rod leading her right toward the dark forest…

Once again, she tossed and turned all night. The soldiers had always been on her list of suspects, but now it seemed they were quickly becoming the *only* suspects. Still, she couldn't very well accuse them of something until she knew what they were doing.

As strange as it sounded, the best course of action was to…venture into the dark forest and keep looking for whatever (or whomever) was draining the river.

So, the next morning after chores, she scouted around for someone who'd be foolish and brave enough to go in with her in broad daylight.

"Absolutely not," Ida said with a firm shake of her head. The butcher had her apron on and was carving up what appeared to be the last remnants of three pigs. "And you're an idiot for wanting to go yourself."

"I don't *want* to go, but I think that's where I'll find the answers I'm looking for," Bev said with a sigh. "Besides that, Allen Mackey's been going for the past week or so."

"Then ask him," she said. "He owes you after all the trouble with the flour."

Flour which remained on his back stoop, untouched, and five gold coins that remained unpaid. "Vicky thinks he's in trouble."

"Then get Vicky to go."

"Why don't you want to?" Bev asked. "You're the strongest person in town. You know how to use those knives. What could you be afraid of?"

Ida put down her knife and glared at Bev. "That's my business, Beverage Wench." She flinched. "We really need to get you a new name. It's hard to stay mad when I call you that."

"Look, at least…" Bev sighed. "If I'm not back by sundown, could you and Vellora maybe come looking for me?"

She let out a sigh. "Are you really serious about going there?"

"It's the next place I need to look. Maybe whoever is draining the river is doing it there—"

"And maybe that person could run you through with a sword," Ida said. "All the more reason to leave it alone."

"The problem will continue until I solve it," Bev said. "So if you're not going with me, I guess I'll just have to go…alone."

Ida released a sigh as Bev slowly moped toward the door. "I won't go with you, but if you're not back by sundown, we'll send a search party." She pointed her knife at Bev. "But you'd *better* be back by sundown, because I don't want to have to explain to my wife why we're embarking on a dangerous mission into a deadly forest."

"You're the best, Ida," Bev said with a smile.

"And for heaven's sake, take a weapon with you!" Ida barked as Bev closed the door behind her.

Bev didn't have much in the way of weapons—and she wasn't about to bring her fine kitchen knife on an adventure into the woods. She dug into the old closet in the stables, hoping maybe Wim McKee had left something useful in there. But it was all bridles and spare saddles, nothing that would help in…whatever trouble Bev was about to get herself into.

With the stable closet a dead-end, she turned to head back to the kitchen as the five soldiers returned. They were *covered* in dirt and mud, but it had an odd orange glow to it. Bev was almost too mesmerized by it to notice that they were traipsing mud into her just-cleaned kitchen.

"Hey!" She ran toward the kitchen. "Can you at least wipe your shoes before you walk inside? I just cleaned."

"Did you?" Karolina asked with a quirked brow. "You tell me you clean every day, but this place is filthy. Our rooms are practically crawling with dust mites."

Bev didn't believe that—the rooms had been spic and span when she'd cleaned them last. "I'd be happy to clean them while you're out."

"There's no need for that," she said. "But I wouldn't scold us again when you obviously can't keep your inn clean on your own. It seems you're… often away."

Bev put her hands on her hips, her anger rising to inhospitable levels. These stupid soldiers might be the cause of all her angst. "That's because I've been stuck trying to figure out why we keep having earthquakes and sinkholes all over town. Someone actually got hurt the other day just sitting in their house. Shocked you haven't noticed or at least *offered* to help."

"Why would we do that? We're here for a purpose, not to resolve the natural inclinations of the land," she said. "I suppose the gnomes were no help."

"They were," Bev said. "They said that someone's…" She stopped herself before she finished that thought. Best not to reveal her cards yet. "Someone's probably behind it. So I'm searching for that someone."

"Well, best of luck, innkeeper. I know you're…" She curled an evil smile. "You're absolutely the *right* person for the job. Much like your brilliant sheriff, who always seems to know exactly what he's doing."

The five soldiers snickered to each other as they walked into the house, none of them wiping their feet as they went. Bev clicked her tongue, trying to dispel her fury and remind herself that these were *paying* customers and they'd paid quite handsomely up until now. Knowing she'd managed to fill her gold bag upstairs took some of the edge off—but not much.

She did have a point, though. Bev *wasn't* the right person for the job. But it seemed she was the only one willing to do it, so she supposed that counted for *something*.

Bev marched into the kitchen and plucked her precious knife from the counter and slipped it into its leather holder. Then she headed out the back door for the dark forest.

CHAPTER SIXTEEN

Even though she carried her trusty knife, Bev's heart pounded nervously as she headed out of town toward the dark forest. The dowsing rod was shoved into the back of her pants and hidden under her shirt, making for an awkward walk, but at least it wouldn't draw any attention. She carried her glowing stick, though since the sun was still out, it was more just a branch covered in mushrooms. She wasn't sure what she'd find in the dark forest, but from a distance, it seemed like the sun didn't get through the thick branches.

Hence the name.

She tried to ignore every tall tale anyone had

ever told her about the place. It was, perhaps, just a thick forest with a bad reputation. Bev was starting to know something about bad reputations, so she could give it the benefit of the doubt.

But as she came closer, something eerie slid over her skin, sending chills down her spine.

"Just me being silly," she said quietly as she tightened her grip on the glowing stick. "Just being silly. Just a forest. Nothing more, nothing less."

The first problem was finding a way in. The brambles grew thick around the tree trunks, rising past Bev's shoulders. She didn't want to hack her way through, but it was starting to look like she might have to. With a heavy sigh, she unsheathed her knife and stared at it.

"I promise I'll take you to get sharpened after all this is over," she said, walking up to the brambles.

But to her surprise, the thicket slid away from her, like a curtain unveiling a dark sky beyond a window. Bev's mouth fell open, and the knife nearly dropped from her hand.

"Um…" She twisted the blade. "Thanks?"

The brambles shivered in response as Bev stepped through the opening and was immediately bathed in darkness. In the absence of light, the mushrooms on her glowing stick became brighter, and she lifted it higher so she could see where she was going as she put away her knife for the moment.

With the brambles parting, the walk was a bit easier, but the forest floor was still covered in thick tree roots that made it tricky to find footing.

The sound of rustling leaves behind her drew her attention, and she gasped as the thicket closed behind her.

"Um, you are going to let me out, right?"

This time, the forest didn't respond at all.

She hadn't a clue how big it was. She didn't travel much outside Pigsend, and she'd only seen the grove from a distance. So she could, perhaps, be walking for days before she found anything. And without sunlight overhead, she didn't have any clue what time it was.

"Perfect, Bev," she repeated. "Just brilliant. You're going to get lost in here. Ida's going to come looking for you so she can wring your neck, then Vellora will wring your neck for putting her wife in danger. Why'd you have to come by yourself anyway? Tons of folks in town who don't think you're the scum of the earth these days." She snorted at her own joke. "Maybe you could've brought one of Rosie's chickens for protection. They seem eager to kill."

She kept moving in what she hoped was the same direction, but it was hard to tell since everything looked exactly the same. Dark trees, hanging vines, thick roots jutting out from the ground. Forward, backward, to the left and to the right, it was all completely identical. If Bev turned the wrong way, she'd be hopelessly lost forever.

"Deep breaths, Bev, old girl," she whispered to herself. "You've probably survived worse than this. Can't remember any of it, but most likely, this isn't the most dangerous thing you've ever done."

It was a good thing she was alone, because if anyone in town caught her talking to herself like this, they might think she was a bit touched in the head.

She stopped, straightening as her good senses finally made a reappearance. She wasn't completely without help—she still had the dowsing rod, which she should've been using to follow the magical river. Tucking the glowing stick under her arm, she put the dowsing rod between her hands.

The tug was immediate, pronounced, and very clearly pulling her forward. Here, at least, the river wasn't blocked—or so she assumed. She still didn't know much about any of this magic stuff.

She took a deep breath and kept walking, sensing the small variations in the way it pulled this way and that as she tried to keep her footing in the jagged roots. How long she'd keep walking, she wasn't sure—nor was she sure what she was looking for in here. It was, however, apparent that the magic was much more potent in this forest—which perhaps meant whoever was siphoning off the river was doing it *close* to—

"Please!"

Bev stopped short, unsure if she'd just heard the wind or an actual someone.

"Don't go. Let me… I'll figure something out."

No, that was definitely a someone. And they sounded like they were in danger.

Bev put the dowsing rod back in her pants and pulled her knife. There was a good chance she'd just stumbled across something she wasn't supposed to, perhaps an unrelated and underhanded deal going on in this dark forest. But curiosity got the better of her, and she kept walking forward.

"…don't have the money for you today."

She stopped in her tracks, her mouth falling open. Was that…*Allen?*

Hesitating, she chewed on her lip. Allen had been going into the forest, but surely…surely the baker's son had nothing to do with the sinkholes. That would be absolutely ridiculous.

Or is it? Had the solution been right under her nose all this time and she hadn't seen it?

"Well, then why did you summon me?"

The other voice was deep, low, smooth as butter. Entrancing might've been a better description, because for a brief moment, Bev thought she'd believe anything that voice said. But she shook her

203

head, clearing the feeling, and silently pushed the last remaining branch out of the way.

"Because I need more of it," Allen replied. "Please. I'm running out of options."

"No money, no help."

Bev finally reached a clearing where Allen stood facing a small…man sitting on a tree stump. Man wasn't really an apt term, but Bev wasn't sure what to call him. He was bigger than the gnomes, but not by much, with large ears that folded over like a dog's and a short, piggy snout complete with bright pink skin. He looked bored to be there, counting gold coins in one hand before switching to another.

"Please," Allen was practically on his knees, "I'm desperate. There has to be something else I can offer you. Something else you want."

"Gold." The creature counted the coins in his hands. "That's it. Surely, the charms I gave you helped you bake some goods, eh?"

Bev's mouth fell open. Allen was buying charms to help him bake? What in the world could he need that for? He just needed to get into the kitchen and get to work.

"I used them, but the cakes and muffins didn't taste the same," he said. "I don't know what I did wrong. I followed my mother's recipe exactly with your magic. And yet it just…" His shoulders slumped. "I can't sell subpar goods. The town will revolt."

"I hardly see how that's my problem. I told you there was a chance it wouldn't work, and you gave me the gold anyway."

"I have to make some money," Allen said, on the verge of tears. "I have debtors coming to call. The miller's banging on my door asking for money, taxes are due to the mayor in a few weeks, and I can't even make a damn dinner roll!"

The creature was unmoved, watching Allen with a wary sort of look.

"I need more magic," Allen said. "I need... Please. Just one more try. Maybe there's a different charm you could use. Or something else that might —"

"Are you telling a magic maker how to do his job?" the creature said, his voice taking on a dangerous tone.

"No, of course not."

"Because if you *were*, I'd tell you to make your own magic. Your mother clearly had some."

"Some, yeah. And took it all for herself," Allen said, almost bitterly. "I got nothing from her. Plain old useless human like my town-skipping father."

Bev frowned. Fernley Mackey had had magic? No wonder her delicacies had been so in-demand. Bev's heart softened for Allen, seeing his slow baking days and snippiness for what it actually was and not what she'd assumed.

"That sounds like a personal problem to me," the creature said, standing. "Now, if you have no gold, I shall be on my way."

"Wait—!"

But the small man disappeared into the air with a loud *pop*, and all that was left was Allen, lurching for the empty stump. Bev moved backward, eager to avoid being seen, but the soft sounds of Allen's sobs caught her by surprise. He fell to his knees, covered his face with his hands, and his entire body was wracked with sobs.

"I'm sorry, Mama," he cried. "I couldn't do what you did. I'm not special like you were. I'm sorry I'm going to lose our home."

Bev couldn't leave him there, couldn't stand to see him in such dire straits. She sighed and stepped out into the clearing.

Allen jumped and spun around, a club in his hand as he searched the dark forest. His gaze landed on Bev, and a mix of shame, anger, and horror flooded his eyes.

"W-what are you doing here? Did you follow me?" He lifted the club. "Get out of here before I —"

"What in the world was that creature you were talking to?" Bev said. "And why were you begging him for magic?"

"None of your damn business," he said, wiping his tears. "Just get out of here. Quit spying on me, or else I'll turn you into Rustin."

"I wasn't following *you*, Allen. I'm trying to find why we've been plagued by sinkholes and the trail led me here. To you." She threw her hands up. "What do you want to tell me about what you've been doing?"

"The sinkholes?" He blinked. "No, I'm not… That has nothing to do with the sinkholes."

"Somebody's draining the magical river," Bev said. "I come here to find it flush with magic, and you buying spells from some kind of…magic dealer. That seems like pretty damning evidence to me."

His shoulders fell. "Maybe it is. He's a magic man. A charmer. You pay him gold in exchange for magical spells. But as you probably saw…they aren't guaranteed to work."

"Why do you need magic in the first place, Allen?" Bev asked. "Baking doesn't require magic. You just combine the ingredients and put it in the oven."

He shook his head. "Not my mom's recipes. They're…different. I do exactly what's on the cards, and I end up with a salty, soggy mess of dough that won't ever set up." He ran his hand over his face. "There was some latent magic in her pots and pans after she died, but it's all gone now. And so…"

"Allen," Bev said with a sigh. "You don't need to be messing with this man. You just need new recipes."

"And then I'll be run out of town," he said. "I tried baking my own stuff once. Made some muffins with a different recipe that I found in a cookbook in the library. Not *one* sold."

Bev vaguely remembered that a few months ago. They lacked that *wow* factor that Allen's mother's goods had. But surely, he could try again with something else. There wasn't much to baking sweets —sugar and butter and flour.

"What kind of magic did she have?" Bev asked.

He lifted his shoulders hopelessly. "She never said. I don't even know if she knew. Maybe she got a line from a parent or grandparent. Otherwise, I would've gotten some, y'know?" He wiped his nose with his elbow. "And I'm as dull as dirt."

"You aren't dull, Allen," Bev said. "You just need to pave your own way."

He sniffed hard. "It's no use. I don't have any money, any prospects. There's no magic in my veins, so…anything I make won't sell. I'll just be baking to toss in the trash."

Bev chewed her lip, staring at the stump. "How does one call this magic man?"

"Why? Need a spell?"

"I just want to talk with him," Bev said. "Ask

him if he knows anything about who might be draining the magical river—and why."

"He won't just come to talk for free. You'll need gold." He sighed. "And as you probably heard, I'm fresh out."

She put her hands on her hips, making a decision. She could spare a bit more gold for this endeavor. "Let's head back to town. If you pay me back, I'll cover your bill with the miller this time. But—"

"There's no point, Bev. I'm going to lose the bakery." He shook his head. "I should just put it up for sale and try to recoup my losses."

"Do you want to keep it?" Bev asked.

He nodded. "It's the only thing I have left of my mom. I couldn't bear to see it in someone else's hands."

"Then we'll save it, together," Bev said. "But first, we've got to make sure these earthquakes stop happening or else the entire town is in danger." She held out her hand. "Deal?"

Allen stared at her hand a long time before he finally took it. "You're a saint, Bev."

"I'm just looking out for Fernley's kid," she said. "Like I promised her I would. But you've got to do something for me in exchange." She nodded to the stump. "I'll give you some gold to bargain with your magic man again. As long as you bring him back so

I can talk with him, too."

He nodded, rubbing his mouth. "He'll be gone for a few hours, at least. Later this afternoon, maybe around four, he'll be available again."

"Then we'll come back at four," Bev said. "Now…how the heck do we get out of this place?"

CHAPTER SEVENTEEN

Allen helped Bev find her way out of the thicket with minimal tears to her clothes, and together, they walked back to town, not a word between them. The bright sunlight of midday was harsh, and Bev had to shield her eyes after being in the dark forest. She wasn't looking forward to going back in there, but for Allen—and her beloved inn—she would.

She glanced at the young man beside her. His cheeks held a small blush as he stared at the ground, like a child who'd been caught in the cookie jar.

"You know," Bev said, after a moment, "I think it's kind of…sweet."

"What?"

"The lengths you're going to in order to stay close to your mom," Bev said. "And save the bakery. It's admirable."

He pursed his lips and said nothing.

"You have a whole bunch of folks who want nothing more than for you to succeed at both. You should ask us for help, if you need it. There's no shame in that."

"I just got...so overwhelmed," he said. "I started losing business and panicked. And I was in too deep to..." He ran a hand through his hair. "And you know, with the soldiers in town, gotta be extra careful talking about anything *magical*." He whispered the word like it was a slur.

"You can trust me," Bev said. "And Vellora and Ida. We'll always have your back, kiddo."

He actually smiled. It seemed like his first one in weeks.

They reached the split between their buildings, and Allen exhaled, looking up at the bakery. "It needs some new paint, you know. Mom would've been furious to see it in such a state."

"Then once all this is taken care of, we'll get some from Earl and see about giving it a fresh coat," Bev said, slapping him on the back. "Now, let's meet back here at four, okay? And we'll put a pin in this nasty business."

He nodded and walked toward the bakery, and

Bev waited until he was inside to head toward the inn. She shook her head as she walked through the back door, musing about what kind of creature that magical man could be. Like the gnomes, it wasn't a great idea for Bev to walk into a negotiation without knowing more about him.

And luckily, she had just the book to tell her the answer—she hoped.

She'd stashed the book of magical creatures under the front desk, so she sat on the stool and hoisted it up, wincing as the loud sound echoed in the empty room. She flipped through the pages, taking her time to scan each drawing for similarities to the magical man on the stump. *Magic Man* wasn't listed anywhere in the book, but she'd guessed that would be the case. It seemed more a title than a type of creature.

She kept a wary eye on the clock—soon she'd need to whip *something* up for dinner, even though she had nothing in her stores.

"Drat," she muttered. She might have to put up a *closed for dinner* sign tonight—something she hadn't done since coming down with a bad case of scoplespox over the winter.

But as she considered whether she could stop looking and run out to the market to nab some potatoes, she'd flipped to a page and was looking at a familiar pig nose.

Barus

A creature of great greed, the Barus lives alone and preys on the desperate. He offers charms and spells to his victims who pay him in gold, but for each subsequent visit, the price increases and the magic becomes less potent until it no longer does what it advertised. The barus will continue to ask for more money until the victim has no more. Best avoided at all costs.

It was as if the author of this book had been in the forest with Bev and Allen. The drawing was so realistic, and the description of behavior was on point. No wonder Allen's charms had stopped working—that was part of the grift, it seemed.

She kept scanning the page, searching for anything about magical siphoning, but she supposed he sourced his charms from the magical river. It was one of the many questions she'd ask him when she saw him later that day. But knowing his game would make it easier to play.

Absentmindedly, she turned the pages of the

book, thinking and strategizing about how she would approach the barus when she stopped, seeing the word *baking* on the current page. The accompanying drawing was of a short creature with a round belly, jovial smile, and tightly coiled blond ringlets. The creature was shown wearing an apron and holding a rolling pin, standing behind a pile of iced cupcakes.

POBYD

The Pobyd is a homemaker creature, closely related to hobgoblins and bwbachons, who thrives in kitchen environments. Their specialty is baking, and they can use their magic to create magnificent confections from basic ingredients.

Bev ran her finger along the drawing, a smile coming to her face. It was plausible, though of course not provable, that this was Fernley's lineage. The creature looked nothing like her, but there was something about the warm smile that seemed familiar. It wouldn't help anything, especially if Allen didn't have the magic himself, but perhaps *knowing* what his mom was might help Allen feel closer to her.

"Innkeeper."

Bev looked up sharply. Karolina stood in front of her, a scrutinizing look on her face. Bev's pulse skipped.

"Still reading that book, I see?" she asked. "The gnomes have moved on. There's nothing you'll find in that book that you need to know."

"Oh, I'm sure," Bev said, trying to keep her voice steady. "Just a bit of light reading to pass the time."

"Have you seen creatures like that in town?" She put her hand on the counter, leaning toward Bev as her sharp eyes flicked down to the pobyd. "Perhaps someone using magic they weren't supposed to?"

"Not lately," Bev replied, sitting back. "Only creatures using magic around these parts are the gnomes. But as you said, they've moved on."

The way the soldier pursed her lips, Bev had a feeling her lie wasn't believed. "I will *remind* you that if you see creatures or magic not under the direction of the queen, it is *required* that you report them to your local sheriff or..." She paused. "Any member of the queen's service."

Bev shifted on the stool. "I'm aware of the law. But this is just a book."

"Then you should, perhaps, read something

else." It wasn't a suggestion. "It's imperative that we keep our lines of magic clear for the approved uses."

"Understood," Bev said, although she didn't really. "Now, what can I do for you today?"

"We will be staying another night." She slid another five coins across the table. "No need for you to make dinner."

"Excellent," Bev replied with a smile. Another vote for closing the inn for the evening. "Have a good night."

The soldier marched up the stairs without another word, and Bev shivered a little as she reopened the book to the pobyd page and placed a small sliver of paper between the pages to mark the place. She'd show Allen when the soldiers had left and when the danger of even being *seen* reading this book had passed. But for now, she walked the book upstairs and hid it in her floorboard along with her savings.

And while she was there, she pocketed another ten coins to bring with her to the forest.

~

"Wow, must be nice to be an innkeeper," Allen said as they walked toward the forest again. He seemed a little lighter than he had a few hours ago, and his eyes had brightened when Bev dangled the coin purse in front of him.

"I'm diving into my savings for this,

technically," Bev said. "So don't take it for granted."

Allen stopped her, putting his hand on her arm. "I'm not. I promise." He put his hands in his pocket. "I...um...made some apple muffins. They weren't half-bad. They weren't like my mom's, but they weren't terrible."

"You know," Bev said with a smile as they came into the clearing, "maybe it's been so long since the townsfolk have had one of your mom's muffins that they might've forgotten how good they tasted."

He snorted. "Don't bet on it."

They approached the clearing and the stump, which was empty. "So what do we do?"

"I need three gold coins," Allen said. "That's the price to call him here."

"Yikes," she said, pulling the coins from her purse.

"It used to be one silver," Allen said. "But you know, his prices keep going up."

Bev nodded knowingly as he put the coins on the stump. She held her breath and waited, hoping that maybe Allen hadn't overstayed his welcome, so to speak, with the creature. But the air shimmered and vibrated around Bev's cheeks as the hair stood up on her neck.

And then, *pop*, the creature appeared holding the three coins.

"Ah, Allen, my boy. Seems you've found a new

line of credit." He stacked the coins and unstacked them in his hand. His dark gaze went from Allen to Bev and his eyes lit up. "Or you've brought me a new friend."

He hopped off the stump and walked over to her, something greedy and dangerous in his face. Bev shifted under his intense gaze as he reached a bony finger up to tug on her shirtsleeve.

"And you are...something else, I can tell." He tilted his head back. "What kind of creature are you? You're fascinating. I must know more about you."

"I'm just an innkeeper," Bev replied with a look as she took a large step back. She didn't think she was anything but ordinary, but she figured he was just trying to lay the charm on thick so she would pay him more gold. "And I have questions for you."

"Answers cost as much as magic," he said, glancing at Allen. "But perhaps I'll give you a small discount. Just one gold coin for—"

Bev flipped the coin over to him. "Are you draining the magic from the river?"

The barus blinked at her, confused. "I'm sure I don't know what you're talking about."

"The magical river that runs through town," Bev said. "It leads here—"

"Of course, that's how I travel from place to place," he said.

"And it's empty in town because someone is

draining it." Bev crossed her arms. "And my current suspect is you."

He burst into laughter. "Oh, you're hilarious. I'm powerful, but I'm not *that* powerful. To drain all the magic from this river would take an ability I do not possess, nor want to possess." He opened his palm, revealing a few multicolored baubles that disappeared when he closed his hand again. "This magic comes from my own body, dear. I don't need to *take* from any river."

Bev wanted to believe he was lying, but she couldn't find a reason for it. "Then who the heck is draining the river?"

"I could give you an answer, but it would cost you another gold coin," he said with a fluttering smile.

"Is it an answer or a guess?" Bev said. "Because a guess is worth a silver."

"Oh-ho! Are you bargaining with me now?" He actually looked amused, not annoyed. For whatever reason, he seemed to think Bev was of a different cloth than Allen. And she was more than happy to let him think so.

Bev shrugged, juggling her coin purse. "I have lots of gold, but little time. So let's not waste either."

He scratched his chin. "It's more of an... explanation. Not an answer. But I can tell something is disrupting, and I can perhaps tell you *why*."

Bev tossed him the gold coin.

"The magical river isn't being drained, it's being *redirected*," he said. "And beyond that, the magic that remains is…foreign, shall we say?"

"What does that mean?" Bev asked, hoping she wouldn't have to pay more.

"Something—or someone—in town is most powerful," he said. "Dangerously powerful. Now, finding such a thing would be quite difficult with all the other magic flooding the area from the river. Too much interference makes for a hard search, you know." He paused, tilting his head. "And so…"

Bev shrugged, not quite following.

He sighed and held out his hand. She tossed him another gold coin.

"And *so*, my educated guess is that someone is looking for the powerful, magical object. And in order to do that, they had to get all the other magic out of the way. Like clearing dirt to find a buried gem. So they've stopped up the magical river to make it easier to search the town."

Bev covered her mouth. Only one group of people would be interested in a powerful, magical object, and they'd been staying at Bev's inn for the past week. She ran her hand through her hair. She'd seen Sheriff Rustin near the forest yesterday, and he said he'd been tasked with keeping the townsfolk away from the forest.

"If that will be all..." the barus said as he hopped back onto his stump.

"One last thing," Bev said, eyeing him. "I've got three gold coins left. I want you to charm Allen to have the power of a pobyd."

"A *what?*" Allen scoffed at the same time the barus began to chuckle.

"And I want a full-strength spell, not one of these half-baked ones you've been giving him for an increased price." She lifted her chin higher. "Or no deal."

"Someone's been doing a bit of research, eh?" He cracked his knuckles. "Fine. One full-strength pobyd charm coming up." He closed his eyes, rubbing his hands together and humming.

"What in the world is a—"

"Shh," Bev said.

The barus opened his mouth, which had begun to glow. And when he closed it, his hands took on the glow for a moment before dimming. He revealed a large green bauble that resembled a giant marble.

"This should do the trick—at least for a few years. It's impossible to do these things forever, mind you. So if you'll be wanting another, you'll need to bring a lot more gold."

"This will just get him by," Bev said, as Allen opened his mouth to respond. "Because we'll be switching him to regular human recipes."

"Suit yourselves."

Allen reached for the bauble but the barus pulled it away. "Gold first."

Bev handed Allen the remaining coins and he gave them to the creature, snatching the bauble as soon as he was able. He held it to his chest like it was the most precious thing in the world.

"It feels like her," he whispered. "Like my mom."

"If that'll be all," the barus said, coming to his feet. "I have more customers in other towns that require my attention." He bowed. "Good day to you both."

And with that, he disappeared with a pop into the darkness.

CHAPTER EIGHTEEN

"How did you know?"

Bev turned to Allen as they walked back into town, the bauble hidden under his cloak. The sun was setting, casting an ethereal glow over the land.

"Know what?"

"What my mom was. What kind of magic she had?"

Bev told him about the encyclopedia, and how she'd found both the barus and the pobyd creatures listed. "But the soldiers staying at the inn came by, and they didn't look too pleased that I was leafing through it. Told me that if I saw any creatures outside the purview of the queen's official list, I was to tell them straight away."

Allen turned to her, his face pale. "And you still…you still helped me?"

"I suppose Vellora is rubbing off on me," Bev said. "Besides that, there's no harm in using magic to make the icing a little sweeter or the rolls a little fluffier." She slowed, turning to him. "But I mean it —once that charm is gone, you've got to switch to regular ol' baking. Understood?"

He nodded. "I think my dabbling with magic makers is over. Not as if I have much money left for them to take, but…" He glanced inside his cloak. "I just can't believe he was able to make this. It feels… It's like she's back with me."

"She never left you, Allen," Bev said softly. "She's the one sitting on my shoulder, making me come bang on your door and keeping you out of trouble."

"Pobyd," he whispered. "That's what she was. A pobyd."

"Don't say that too loudly," Bev said as they walked into town. "Now hear me and hear me good: Go back to your bakery and keep that thing hidden at all costs, okay? Just bake to your little heart's content."

"Why? What are you going to do?"

Bev didn't want to say. She didn't even want to *think* it, lest the soldiers could mind-read.

"Continue my investigation, I suppose."

"If you need any help, I'm yours," Allen said, holding out his hand to shake hers. "It's the least I can do after all you've done for me. It's more than I deserved, I'll tell you that much."

She smiled. "I'll be sure to let you know if I do."

She would've loved to have help, but Allen was already too close to magic to risk him getting more involved. This was going to have to be an investigation she continued on her own.

"Just get home," Bev said. "And stay out of trouble."

⁓

Although she didn't want to, Bev placed the *Closed for Dinner* sign on the back doorknob. Then she sat down at her kitchen table with a cup of tea and began to strategize.

She had several options, of course. She, herself, could look for the powerful magical object, but she didn't have the faintest idea where to find such a thing and if she were caught with it, the soldiers might accuse her of having had it all along.

Then again, it might not be an object at all. The soldiers could be in town hunting for a particular townsperson. Of course, no one jumped out at her as a mega powerful being, but what did she know? There seemed to be magic sprinkled throughout the Pigsend population. It stood to reason one of them might be hiding more than they let on.

No, finding the object or person seemed like a bad idea. Best to let those sleeping dogs lie.

Another option could be to destroy the magical dam that was somewhere between the town and the dark forest. That would, essentially, fix the pressing issue of disruptions to the earth and at least buy her more time. But the soldiers would most likely construct another one and—worse, they could seek retribution from the townsfolk for messing with their business.

If she was going to go to Hendry, she needed to have some proof—real proof—that the soldiers were responsible. But where the heck would she find such evidence?

She tilted her head up, thinking about the five rooms where the soldiers had been sleeping over the past week. Entering a tenant's room without permission was a hard no-no—Wim McKee had drilled that into her head. Not that she'd ever had a hankering to do it.

It was almost seven in the evening. She didn't know when they'd be back, but they usually didn't come back until late. If she was going to act, she'd have to do it *now*.

As if being pushed by a force outside her body, she rose and walked out into the main room. In the front desk drawer, there was a master key, able to unlock any room in the inn. Usually it was reserved for absentminded tenants misplacing their room key or locking themselves out, but in this case…

"What am I doing?" Bev whispered, putting the key down. Wim would be—

Wim would be proud of you for following through. The voice was clear.

She snatched the key from the drawer and headed up the stairs.

The closer she came to the room, the less sure of herself she became. She stopped in front of the first bedroom, pressing her ear to the door and listening. Once she didn't hear anyone on the other side, she slipped the master key into the lock and turned it, letting herself into the room.

Each room in the inn was more or less the same. Two twin beds, one pressed against either wall, a center window with red drapes that could block out most of the sun, and a dark blue rug on the floor. A small table between the window held a lantern and a chest of drawers against either wall for those who decided to stay awhile.

Bev scanned the room. There wasn't much evidence that someone had been staying here at all, let alone for a week. The only clues were that the pillow on one of the beds had been tucked under the quilt, instead of laid on top, and a spare uniform hung from the peg on the door. Bev checked the drawers; they were empty. After a few minutes of snooping, she came to the conclusion that whatever the soldiers had brought to Pigsend, they carried with them on their nightly escapades.

With that room a dead end, Bev let herself out, locking the door behind her, and tried the next room over. It was much the same as the first—sparse with only a spare uniform, bed made with the pillow tucked under the blanket. She moved swiftly, knowing at any moment, the soldiers could return.

Finally, she came into what had to be Karolina's room. Not only did the uniform hanging on the door bear her rank, but there was a diary sitting on the bedside table, along with a travel pen and ink.

Bev hesitated. Mucking around in a bedroom was one thing, but reading her diary seemed like a breach of trust. There wasn't anything else worth looking at though, and if she wanted to make this dangerous mission worth it…

Wincing, she opened the journal and flipped to the page marked with the small ribbon.

Another day in this disgusting town.

Well, that didn't bode well.

Every day we don't complete our mission is another

day stuck in this horrific place, away from my beloved Adelard. My heart is empty without him, my bed feels too big, and my arms ache for him to be returned to me. My soul is as untethered as a ship in a storm...

Bev wouldn't have expected a soldier like Karolina to have left details of her mission lying around, but to see such flowery passages about a beloved…something (Bev kept reading a ways. It was hard to tell if she was referring to a person or pet). Perhaps even the mean old soldier had a soft spot.

Leaving the ribbon in its place, she flipped to the front of the book, reading from the first page. It was dated almost a year ago, in a town called Twiddleston.

The earthquakes are getting worse here, but we must carry on. Arnett informs me that what we're looking for is sure to be here, though I'm not sure I believe her. There are so many powerful artifacts scattered across the continent after the war. We could be honing in on something else, entirely.

I just wish to be home with Adelard. He is...

"That's enough of that," Bev said, turning the page on Karolina waxing poetic. She flipped a couple pages until she found another entry dated two weeks later.

Twiddleston is no more. The cracks in the earth seem to have been too much for the sea town, and it fell down the cliffside. No telling how many perished; that's not our job. But with the damage, it's too much for us to continue our search here. So Arnett is following another trail to see where it leads us.

Another month away from Adelard. My heart is...

Bev swallowed. A whole town sank into the ocean? She didn't want to jump to conclusions, but the evidence seemed pretty clear that the soldiers had been doing the same thing to Twiddleston as Pigsend—and didn't seem to care one bit about the consequences. Karolina couldn't spare more than a few words for those in the city, and Bev had to assume the casualties were immense. Even if, by some miracle, they weren't, an entire city was effectively wiped off the map.

She was so caught up in her thoughts that she almost didn't hear the sound of footsteps climbing up the stairwell. Scrambling, Bev closed the journal, ensuring it was exactly as she'd found it. Then she looked left, right. She was trapped inside the room. Just as the doorknob was turning, she dove under the second bed.

Two pairs of filthy boots walked into the room. Bev's heart was pounding so loudly, the soldiers would surely hear. But they seemed too engrossed in their own argument to notice anything else.

"This is taking entirely too long." Karolina sounded angry. "The queen will be expecting an update, and we have nothing to give her."

"Maybe we should move the diverter farther up the river," replied one of the other soldiers. "More magic is seeping through and messing with our dowsing rods."

Dowsing rods? So they were using the same tool as Bev? Good thing she hadn't advertised hers.

"Or maybe we've been led on a mission to nowhere." Karolina released a loud sigh. "If we don't find it tonight, I'm dragging every one of these filthy townsfolk out of their houses and questioning them one-by-one. Starting with that obnoxious innkeeper. I think she knows more than she's letting on."

Bev shivered then froze, hoping they hadn't heard her.

"Our orders were to keep this under wraps," the other soldier replied. "It's vital no one knows what we're looking for, lest they try to keep it hidden."

"I know what our orders are," Karolina snapped. "But something needs to happen, or we'll be stuck in this pigsty forever." She huffed. "And I'm not sure how much longer this town can stand having their river dammed up like this. Another earthquake and the whole place might go under. I don't think I need to remind you of what happened in Twiddleston."

Bev's heart skipped, and she sucked in a silent breath. Could Pigsend completely disappear like Twiddleston had? There wasn't a sea, but the ground itself could swallow the town.

Bev couldn't let it happen. No matter what, she would protect this town.

"No, ma'am, you don't," the soldier responded. "But our finders were certain that it's here. So we shouldn't give up hope. Perhaps tonight's the night it'll turn up."

"Mm. You've said that before." The shiny black boots crossed the room. "Maybe you want to recalibrate your finders, then. You have one more night before I take things into my own hands."

The soldier waited a breath before answering. "Yes, ma'am."

They left together, and Bev waited at least fifteen minutes before crawling out from beneath the bed. Her hands shook as she locked the door behind her and hurried down to her own room, closing the door and pressing herself against it while she took calming breaths.

She was certainly not cut out for this sort of clandestine nonsense. But the love she had for this beautiful little town…that was too much for her to ignore.

As her pulse quieted to normal, she opened her eyes. There was *some* proof. She'd heard them with her own ears. Would it be enough for Hendry to do anything about it? Bev didn't know, but at this point, she had to try. As Karolina had said, the town's days were numbered the longer they left their…diverter in place. Bev could return to Karolina's room, swipe the diary, and—

She felt the air move before the ground. Every instinct in her body told her to *get out of the inn* as the floors began to twist and groan. Bev dashed down the stairs as the walls shivered and dust fell from the ceiling. She struggled to keep her footing through the kitchen, wincing as her precious pots and pans fell from their hangers onto the ground. And finally, she made it out to safety as a loud *crack* echoed around her.

She spun around, sensing something was wrong but not seeing it.

"Bev!" Ida called from around front. "Bev! Come quick!"

She closed her eyes, already knowing what she would see as she rounded the corner. The front of the inn had fallen into the sinkhole. It was a clean break, revealing the front room, complete with Bev's counter and the long dining table where she hosted her nightly meals. Wide open for the world to see. On the second floor, two rooms on either side were also visible. The beds, drawers, lamps…exactly as they'd been in the moments before when Bev had been sneaking around in them. Just the front wall and windows had disappeared.

"Oh, Bev," Ida said, resting a gentle hand on her friend's shoulder. "I'm so sorry."

Bev couldn't find the words, so she just held her hand over her mouth and stared in stunned silence at the gaping hole where her front door used to be.

Chapter Nineteen

"Here's your sign."

Vellora dusted off the wooden sign with *The Weary Dragon Inn* carved into it. It had been hanging over the front door as long as Bev had been there.

Bev swallowed hard as she took it in her hands. "Thanks," she said numbly.

"The sign's in good shape," Ida said, putting her hand gently on Bev's shoulder. "I'm sure you can hang it again once everything's back to normal."

"And it will get back to normal," Allen said, though he sounded less sure than Ida had. "Earl said it was all fixable."

That was true. The carpenter had stopped in to check on things and had done a quick assessment of the damage. Even so, everything felt so overwhelming, Bev didn't even know where to begin.

The butchers and Allen had come over right away and got to work trying to salvage... Bev didn't even know. Memories? Bricks? Anything that might make Bev feel like she hadn't just wasted two weeks running around doing everything except looking into the people staying under her nose. Perhaps if she'd just gone searching for their magical dam instead of snooping in their bedrooms, she might've been able to prevent this.

"You can rebuild," Vellora said. "It'll be even better than before, too. That's what Earl said, remember?"

Bev couldn't find it in herself to be optimistic. No one else in town had come to help, or even offer their sincere apologies for what had happened. In their minds, this was warranted.

"What a mess."

Bev looked up as Karolina and the four soldiers came walking up, looking down into the hole. Vellora made a noise of anger, but Ida shushed her.

"We'll get it fixed," Ida replied when Bev said nothing.

"I'm sure you'll do your best," Karolina replied

with a sneer. "Say, innkeeper, is the place structurally sound? Would hate to waste gold on a place that lacks a front door, you know."

"Why don't you lay off, eh?" Vellora snarled. "Can't you see she's in mourning?"

"I can't, actually. You're filthy." The soldier sniffed. "My two soldiers will double up. Tomorrow, we'll pay you three pieces of gold." She smirked. "Since there are only three rooms available to us."

They walked away, and Vellora balled her fists. "I'm going to murder that—"

"Be nice," Ida chided. "You don't want to draw attention to yourself."

"Don't give them another thought, Bev," Allen said. "Their gold will go toward rebuilding the inn."

"I don't know if there's anything else to salvage," Bev said, her throat raw and sore. "I think we should just…call it a night. Maybe things won't look so bleak in the morning."

"I'm just across the street," Allen said, taking Bev's hand. "Anything you need, just ask."

He turned and left them, and Ida let out a low whistle. "Did someone hit that boy on the head, or…?"

"It's a long story," Bev said, rubbing her forehead. "And it's been a long day."

Ida smiled warmly. "Why don't you come to our place and sleep on the couch, eh?"

"No." Bev shook her head. "Thank you, though. I feel like…I need to stay with the old girl."

"Then go get some rest," Vellora said. "You need your strength."

Bev nodded. "I will. But I need to go talk with Hendry about this. Enough is enough."

Ida and Vellora shared a look of concern. "What are you talking about?" Vellora asked.

"I think…" Bev said, dropping her voice. "I think the soldiers *are* behind this."

Vellora wore a smirk of triumph, but Ida just grew more worried. "Bev, are you sure *Hendry* is the one you want to seek help from? She works for the queen, too."

Bev sighed. It was a risk, for sure. Hendry might hear Bev's explanation and immediately call the soldiers to take her away. But at this point, with the inn nearly destroyed, there wasn't much left for her to lose.

"It's the only thing I have," she said.

"If you think that's best," Ida said, her brow still furrowed in concern. "Come by in the morning and have a cuppa." She pulled Bev in for a squeeze that was a little harder than it should've been. "And don't make me come looking for you, either, Beverage Wench."

Bev walked across town as fast as she could,

finding the mayor's little home tucked between several others on the north side of town. She had to bang on the front door a few times before Hendry answered. Even in the dead of night, she looked put together and magnificent, her lips that brilliant color red. Did she just *look* like that all day long?

"Bev, I swear, if you woke me up just to gawk at me…"

"Sorry." She shook her head. "There was another earthquake—"

"I felt it."

"The inn has…partially collapsed."

Hendry opened her door wider, her hand coming to her mouth. "Oh, Bev. I'm so sorry to hear that." She looked genuinely upset. "In the morning, we'll pull the townsfolk together and—"

"I don't think any of them will help," Bev said. "Some of them might even say I deserved it for not moving faster to find the cause of the earthquakes."

She tutted. "Some might. But you know, these natural disasters are so very random. It's—"

"They're not random," Bev said, looking up. "That's the thing. I know…" She licked her lips, tasting dirt. "I know what's causing them—and who."

"Then why haven't you spoken up sooner?" Hendry said. "You could've saved us all a lot of aggravation."

"Because when I tell you what's going on…" She shook her head. "We might want to step inside for this."

Hendry opened her door wider and allowed Bev entry. Her house was quaint and neat, the perfect abode for a fastidious mayor who didn't seem to care much for frills except those to enhance her appearance. She led Bev to a small table in her homey kitchen and walked to the hearth to poke at the still-smoldering embers.

"I don't think it'll be enough for tea—" She began.

"No need. I just have to get this out." Bev took a breath. "It's the queen's soldiers."

Hendry spun around. "What?"

"They're the ones who are…" She licked her lips. "They're here for something—or someone—powerful. So they've dammed up the magical river that runs beneath the town to clear the air, so to speak, and make it easier to find. The lack of magic has been causing the earthquakes."

Hendry stared at her silently. Then she crossed the small kitchen and sat down opposite Bev. "What in the good green earth are you talking about?"

For what felt like the hundredth time, Bev explained the concept of the magical river and how disrupting it had caused the earthquakes. She left out the parts about Allen and the magic man, Merv and the dowsing rod, and anything else that might end up implicating anyone innocent.

Hendry listened intently, saying nothing until Bev had finished her story. "Do you...do you understand what you're saying here? You're accusing the *queen's soldiers* of destroying the town as they search for magic."

"I know," Bev said with a nod.

"Even if they are, Bev..." She shook her head. "You know that I work for the queen, right? It's a very *long* chain of command, of course. But it's still there. Those soldiers aren't... I'm not at liberty to order them around."

Bev leaned forward. "I...uh...*overheard* them talking about another town on the coast. The entire thing just sank into the sea after a series of earthquakes. That's going to happen to Pigsend if we aren't careful."

Hendry was silent, staring at her perfectly shaped fingernails. Bev couldn't assess what was going on in her mind, as the mayor had a habit of shifting with the prevailing winds. Surely, *surely*, her love of the town would usurp her loyalty to the queen. She seemed to always want to be the most liked, the most popular person—and Pigsend was here. The queen was in some far-off castle.

"I'm not going to be able to help you," Hendry said, slowly, quietly, almost too low for Bev to hear.

"You can't be serious—"

"The soldiers would throw *me* in chains if I did," she said, holding up her hands. "However, I'm sure with this new earthquake, there will be a request for another town meeting." She tilted her head, glancing outside as if she could read the minds of the people sleeping beyond. "Rosie's been hinting that she'll call one every day until the earthquakes are done."

"I'm sure she has," Bev muttered.

"Right now, all you have is hearsay. Conversations and discussions that only you've heard, right?" Bev nodded. "That's easily dismissed. The soldier's words against yours, and the soldiers will probably win." She lifted a finger. "*But* if you were to bring proof—real, definitive proof that they're behind the earthquakes—to a town meeting..." She lifted a shoulder. "A room full of people might be a bit more persuasive than one mayor and one innkeeper."

"How the heck am I supposed to do that?" She could steal Karolina's diary, but that might put her in *more* hot water than just accusing them. "I'm not even allowed to talk about the magical river to people, lest I run afoul of the queen's rules."

"I don't envy your task," Hendry said, rising and gesturing toward the door. "But my hands are tied. If you want to stop them, you're going to have to do it on your own."

Dazed, Bev rose (though not of her own volition) and walked out of Hendry's house. She didn't stop walking, nor did she feel in control of her own body, until she was standing at her back door, staring at the *Closed for Dinner* sign. She shook herself, turning around and putting her hand over her mouth.

"That weaselly little..." She ran her hand through her hair. Some mayor! Just kicking the can down the road and putting everything on Bev to fix. And clearly hiding a little magic of her own.

But as she walked through the inn, seeing the cracks in the plaster on the remaining walls and the cool breeze that blew unabated through the missing one, it was clear this wasn't a task that could go to just anyone. Somehow, in some way, Bev was uniquely suited to solving this problem.

And darn it all if she wasn't going to solve it.

Tending to the horses and Sin felt normal, so when Bev awoke, she set to the chores she could accomplish while missing the front wall to the inn. Though it was a bit degrading to muck the soldiers' horses' stalls, knowing they were responsible for Bev's bad mood and broken home.

She was just about done when Ida called her name. The butcher rounded the corner with a cup of tea and a muffin. She saw Bev and her entire face brightened.

"Courtesy of a weirdly joyful Allen," she said, handing the muffin to Bev. She took a hearty bite and immediately tasted the presence of the pobyd magic. The blueberries were succulent, the sugar just perfect, and even though the muffin was cool to the touch, it melted in her mouth like it was right out of the oven.

"Amazing," Bev said, a little sadly.

"He saw me headed this way and wanted to make sure you had breakfast," she said. "Are you two…good now?"

"I suppose." Bev took the cup. "As good as I can be with anyone in town."

"How did it go with Hendry?" Ida asked.

Bev sighed, staring off into space and told Ida about the soldiers, and her conversation with Hendry. Ida's eyes grew wider as the story went on, and she practically stomped the ground when Bev told her the mayor was powerless.

"So what? Is she just going to let them run roughshod across the town until it shakes into nothing?" Ida barked, a little louder than Bev would've liked.

"Keep your voice down." Bev held out her hands. "They're asleep upstairs."

Ida pursed her lips. "And? They're guilty. Bring

it before the town."

"Hendry doesn't think it'll matter unless I have actual proof," Bev said with a shrug. "Something that'll convince the town of their guilt. Hendry seemed to believe that if *everybody* in Pigsend stood against the soldiers, they would be too overwhelmed and leave."

Ida rubbed her chin. "As much as I hate to admit it, she does…have a good point. So we need undeniable proof of their guilt so we can cause a good, old-fashioned town riot." She glanced at Bev. "Do you have anything?"

"Nothing I can use."

"Well, what is it?"

Bev glanced up, praying no one was listening in as she lowered her voice to barely above a whisper. "Well, last night, before the earthquake, I snuck into the soldiers' rooms—"

"Beverage Wench! You naughty girl," Ida said with a grin. "What'd you find? Sacrifices to Queen Meanie? Self-flagellation whips?"

"Nothing much," Bev said with a chuckle. "Just a…" She glanced around again, lowering her voice. "Diary."

"That sounds promising," Ida said. "Why can't you use that as proof, again?"

"Well, I don't really want to advertise that the proprietor of the Weary Dragon Inn is in the habit of snooping on her tenants, even if she had a good reason," Bev said. "So I need to find something else."

"I'll help you." Ida tapped her chin. "You said they're damming up the river? What if we go find evidence of the dam?"

"We could try that," Bev said. "I have a general idea where it is, but I'm not completely sure." She rubbed her chin. "And we'd run the risk of the soldiers catching us in broad daylight."

"*But* if we destroyed their dam, we could also stop more earthquakes," Ida said. "Right?"

Bev nodded.

"One more shake, Bev, and your inn is done for. Maybe our butcher shop, too. We don't have time to waste."

Bev watched her dear friend, as guilt and foreboding crawled up her spine. "Are you sure you want to get involved in this, Ida? What if..." She rubbed her hands together. "What if the soldiers find us and arrest us? What if you..." She didn't want to come right out and say it, but she feared what would happen if the soldiers noticed Ida's supernatural strength. "It's a big risk for you, too. Maybe you should discuss it with Vellora."

"Discuss what with me?" Vellora walked around the corner holding an entire basket of muffins. "Allen said to bring these by. Told me to tell you they were a slightly different recipe and he wanted your opinion."

Bev and Ida took a muffin each. Immediately, Bev knew there was no magic in the mix, but...it didn't need it. The blueberries were warm and juicy, the sugar perfectly laid on top. And just like the other one, it melted in her mouth.

"Whatever you did to Allen," Vellora said, stuffing another muffin into her mouth, "fank ew on be'hawf of the west uf us." She swallowed. "Now what kind of mischief are you two getting into?"

"I'll tell you the details later," Ida said. "But the short version is that we might have a way to stop the earthquakes and kick the soldiers out of town. Just need to do some hunting today. Can you watch the shop while I go with Bev?"

"Sorry, love," Vellora said, swallowing the muffins. "I come with good muffins and bad tidings. Rosie's called for a town meeting. Like..."

The bell in town chimed ten.

"Now."

Chapter Twenty

In usual times, Bev wouldn't have been required to attend the town meeting. But Rosie had asked for an update *by name*, so she had no choice but to follow the butchers toward the town hall. Vicky came out of the seamstress shop, giving Bev a nervous look. Down the street, Etheldra was talking with Earl and Jane and eyed Bev meanly.

"Mixed bag today," Ida muttered.

"We've got to figure out how to get out of this thing quickly," Bev said. "Maybe I can just tell them I've got nothing, and we can call it a day."

"You know that's not how it's going to go," Vellora said. "Everyone's going to have an opinion, and everyone's going to be able to talk."

Bev sighed as she walked into the main space, feeling angry gazes from most of the crowd. Allen, at least, gave her a small, hopeful thumbs-up, with Vicky by his side. But there was a dearth of friendly faces in what should've been a sea of them.

She continued the long walk up the center, finding her spot between Rustin and Hendry's empty seat. Rustin actually looked somber enough for the occasion, giving her a muted smile as she sat.

"It's not so bad," he said. "You get used to being yelled at."

"I doubt it," Bev said. "But thanks." She paused, giving him a look. "Say, if you're here, who's watching the soldiers'...whatever?"

He shrugged. "Good question."

"Have they still told you nothing about what they're doing?"

"No, I think they find me a little dim, you know?" He chuckled. "But joke's on them. Eventually, they'll move on to another town, and I'll get to sleep in my own bed tonight. Something to be said for being a soldier in a town versus on Her Majesty's Special Squad."

Bev tried not to look too interested. "They're on a special squad? What's that?"

"It's just a name for what they do. Get their orders direct from the queen. Gives them the ability to order everyone else around—even Mayor Hendry!"

Bev chewed her lip. That certainly explained Hendry's reluctance to deal with them directly. "Still have you on the road to the dark forest?"

"They've had me a few places." He began rattling off a couple farmlands and locations on his fingers. Bev listened with a frown. Maybe there were multiple points where the river flowed into the city, and they were moving the dam around? That would take much longer than just walking around the perimeter of the dark forest. "Just standing around all day until well after the sun goes down." He yawned. "I tell you, these late nights'll get ya."

"Have they put you anywhere near one of the sinkholes?"

"Oh, Bev, if they had me doing that, I surely would've mentioned it!" He let out a laugh. "Don't be silly. How in the world could they be responsible for the earthquakes? They're just here doing whatever they're doing for the queen." He put his hands on his stomach, still chuckling. "What a funny thought."

Bev forced a tight smile. "Yes, hilarious."

She didn't have time to chew on that thought because Hendry walked out of her office, her raven hair swinging behind her back as she wordlessly approached the table. Bev was pleased, at least, to see that she looked like she hadn't gotten much sleep, but she still had the radiant look of a woman who always had herself together.

With a sigh, Hendry stood in front of her chair and held up her hands to quiet the crowd.

"My dear friends," she said, plastering on a smile that looked fake up close, "we are here…*yet again* to discuss the matter of the sinkholes. Rosie Kelooke has called this town meeting, asking for Bev to give us an update on her investigation progress. So with that, I turn the floor over to Bev." She glanced at Bev. "Who I'm sure will provide any evidence she has discovered before she declares any suspects."

Bev pursed her lips. She hated to lie, but she didn't have a choice. "I have no evidence nor suspects. That's your update today."

The room erupted into loud cries of anger as the townsfolk came to their feet. Bardoff had his fist in the air, while Apolinary was almost climbing over her seat. Rosie just shook her head while even Earl and Jane looked put out by the news. In the back, Vellora and Ida watched helplessly.

"Calm yourselves," Hendry said, holding up her (Bev was convinced) magical hands. The townsfolk sat down in their chairs. "We will conduct this town meeting respectfully and in accordance with our laws and customs. Understood?"

They did, but they didn't look happy about it.

"Now," Hendry straightened, "who would like to go first?"

Unlike most every town meeting Bev had been to in the past five years, this one remained annoyingly on topic. Bev found herself answering questions about the gnomes and what they'd told her over and over again, because that was the only thing she was comfortable talking about. Everything else was too far into the "magical" realm, and she wanted to keep that close to the vest.

The hours ticked by, and Bev couldn't help but watch the clock every time another townsperson came up to speak. She'd never felt like there was a timeline, though she was eager to get the earthquakes resolved quickly. But since finding out what had happened to Twiddleston, and that the last earthquake had taken more of the inn, she wanted to get out and find her proof *today.*

"That question has already been asked, Mr. Silver," Hendry said. "Several times, in fact. I believe Bev has answered it satisfactorily. Does anyone have anything *new* to add? Otherwise, we can all go back to our normal days and let Bev continue her investigation."

"I have something to say."

Rosie had been quiet, considering she'd been the one to call the town meeting in the first place. She shimmied out of the crowd, walking slowly up the center to stand before the front table. Her wizened face was screwed into a sour expression, her hands resting on a cane as she narrowed her gaze at Bev.

"Very well, Rosie," Hendry said, sounding exhausted. "What's your question?"

The old woman adjusted her shawl across her body and lifted her chin as she spoke. "Bev, I would like to ask you the one question I haven't yet heard." She paused, inhaling and exhaling, perhaps for effect. "Are *you* the one behind the sinkholes?"

Bev sat up, her brows shooting upward. "Are you…joking?"

"I'm as serious as the Harvest Festival pie competition," she said. "Are you the one who's causing these earthquakes?"

Bev opened and closed her mouth, unsure how to respond to that. Finally, she blurted, "And how would *I* be responsible for earthquakes and sinkholes? And *why*?"

"Because you're eager to rebuild the inn and get money for it!" Rosie said, pointing her old, bony finger at Bev. "And in your devious plot to destroy your inn, you're taking the whole town with you. It's the only explanation for why you've been *so eager* to take on this investigation, despite Sheriff Rustin already being on the case."

"He hasn't been *on* the case because he's been

following the queen's soldiers around," Bev drawled. "And this is ridiculous. I'm invested because *my home* is about to fall into a pit!"

"I agree with Rosie!" Trent Scrawl rose as he called out into the crowd. "She's been skulking about. Accusing innocent people of doing things to hurt the town. It wouldn't surprise me if *she* was the one doing it!"

"How much do we know about *Bev* anyway?" Stella Brewer cried. "If that's even your real name."

"It's not, actually," Bev said, a little dryly. "Remember? I came into town without a memory?"

"A likely story," Rosie drawled. "I think we should investigate *Bev* and what she's been up to!"

"I bet she's been lying about losing her memory, too!"

"She's a wolf in sheep's clothing!"

A raucous chorus of approval echoed through the space, and Bev's pulse raced. She turned to Hendry, hoping for an assist, but it seemed the mayor was content to allow chaos to reign.

"How would I cause earthquakes?" Bev barked. "I don't have magic. I'm not powerf—"

A loud, rhythmic thumping noise echoing underneath the crowd. Slowly, more in the room began to hear it too, quieting their tirades against Bev to listen. They stared at each other, at the window, at the backdoor…

Where a large shadow was blocking out the sun.

Hendry rose slowly, a furrow on her brow. "What in the…"

There was a familiar grunting as the shadow squeezed through the doorway, barely fitting and having to duck his furry head. He wore a knitted eye mask, but he navigated the room with ease, perhaps just by smell, sound, and the feel of his long claws on the floor. As he passed, each townsfolk wore a similar look of horror, amazement, disgust, shock. Even Hendry looked like she'd never seen such a thing in her entire life.

"I told you! I told you they existed!" Eldred Nest jumped up and down. "You all thought I was crazy! Well, who's crazy now?"

Merv finished his long walk to the front of the room and stood three feet from Bev, Hendry, and Rustin. "I understand that these sorts of town meetings are designed to let everyone say their piece," he announced loudly. "And so I would like to do the same."

"W…What in the good green earth are you?" Hendry blurted after a moment.

"My name is Merv," he said, his voice echoing in the space. "I live nearby. And I've come to *respectfully* ask that you topsiders *stop* whatever you're doing because *my entire home* is about to collapse!"

Not a word was spoken in the room as Merv stood there, whiskers twitching, looking somewhat ridiculous with two large purple knitted patches over his eyes. Bev wasn't sure what to say, but she slowly rose to her feet.

"Mayor, townspeople of Pigsend," she said. "This is Merv. He…uh…lives near here."

"That's what I said," the mole huffed. "Nice to see you again, Bev."

"Bev?" Hendry turned to her. "You know this… this thing?"

"He's not a thing," Bev said. "He's a… Well, as he said, he lives near here. Underground. And—"

"So *he's* the one who's been causing these earthquakes?" Rosie stood up and pointed at him.

"Oh, don't be—" Merv began, but the townsfolk drowned him out with angry shouting.

Bev looked at Hendry, hoping the mayor would intervene, but she just put her hands in her lap as she sat back down.

"Do something," Bev said. "They're going to…" Bev didn't consider anyone in town violent, but they certainly sounded like they could be. "He didn't *do* anything."

"I would think, Bev, you'd be happy to no longer be the prime suspect," Hendry said with a look.

"Yes, except it doesn't *solve the problem*," she

said. "Which is still going to be a problem if we don't do something, like, today."

"Then I apologize for what I'm about to do," Hendry said. "But I think you'll see the reason and thank me for it."

She rose and held up her hands, quieting the angry conversations with a look.

"Well, I'll be," Hendry said. "It appears our suspect has made himself known."

"*Suspect*?" Bev and Merv said at the same time, both looking concerned.

"And since we're all gathered here, I think we should convert this town meeting into an official town trial."

Bev jumped to her feet, horrified. "Hendry, you *can't* be serious. Merv is innocent. He's lived here for—"

"Bev, you're free to go, unless you'd like to stay and defend Merv." Hendry's eyes said more than she could publicly.

Bev licked her lips, looking at Merv, torn. "Are you saying—"

"You can stay, or you can go do whatever you were doing earlier," she said. "But today, the townsfolk will be putting this creature on trial for the crime of causing sinkholes in town."

~

A town trial was much like a town meeting,

except much rarer, usually happening when two neighbors couldn't settle their differences or someone in town was accused of a crime. Much like the regular town meeting, everyone was allowed to question both parties, then a vote was held on the outcome.

"Well, I just don't see why this is necessary," Merv said after Bev explained all this to him. "I'm not guilty of anything."

"We know," Bev said. There was a brief recess between the meeting and the trial, so Bev had guided Merv to a corner to have a chat, and Ida and Vellora had followed. "But I think this is just a distraction so we can go find the real suspects."

"I don't see why I've been dragged into it." Merv bristled.

"Because Hendry needs a scapegoat," Bev said. "And unfortunately, you're the only one with a… coat. So."

Merv turned to Vellora, who hadn't spoken or stopped staring since they'd walked over. "Can you please stop gawking at me?"

"I've just… Are you real?"

"As real as you are," he said. "And regretting leaving my home. But you know, Bev, I thought, when we'd talked—"

"I know," Bev said. "And I'm sorry. But if you'll just stall the townsfolk long enough for us to find the proof we're looking for, I promise, we'll clear the air. And hey, maybe I'll buy five blankets from you."

"Oh, pshaw, they're not worth buying," he said, but he actually looked like he was blushing. "Fine. I'll play along with this ridiculous sideshow. But only if you promise you aren't leaving me out to dry."

"I promise," Bev said, taking his oversized paw and squeezing it. "Ida, Vellora—"

Ida nodded. "Vel, you stay here and monitor things. If we take too long, we need you to stall the crowd. Just start asking inane questions about nothing. Or complain about someone. You know, the usual."

"The two of you can't go alone," Vellora said, seeming to snap out of her reverie.

"Then I'll go, too."

Allen Mackey stood behind them, wringing his hands. "I don't know what we're doing, but I owe Bev a debt of gratitude. So whatever trouble you're getting into, I'm getting into it with you."

Bev sighed. She would much rather have gone alone, but she couldn't deny that it was nice to have a few friendly faces in her corner.

"We'll be back as soon as we can, Merv," Bev said. "Just hang on. And whatever you do, don't admit that you've done *anything* until we get back."

Chapter Twenty~One

Even though Bev didn't want to leave Merv, she had a bigger purpose in mind. After a quick stop at the inn to grab her magical dowsing rod, Bev, Ida, and Allen hurried out of town toward the dark forest. Bev wasn't even sure they'd find anything there, but it was the best place to start.

"When I saw Rustin, he was on that road," Bev said. "But from what he said, they've got him moving around. So I'm not sure that's where we'll find the dam." She glanced to the others. "Or maybe there's more than one?"

"Let's hope not," Ida said. "There's a lot of ground to cover and not a lot of time. I don't know how long Merv and the others will be able to stall."

"So…Merv," Allen said, slowly. "He's like…real. Right? I didn't imagine a giant mole man?"

"Very real. I've been to his house," Bev said with a smile.

"Let's hope we can clear his name," Ida said as the dark forest appeared over the hill. She slowed her gait, putting her hand to her head as she looked left and right at the farms that stretched as far as the eye could see. "Where the heck do we even begin to look?"

"Well, that's why I brought this." Bev pulled the dowsing rod from the back of her pants and waved it in the air. "I'm hoping it'll lead us to the dam."

"A stick?" Ida frowned. "Are you sure that's…"

"It's called a dowsing rod," Bev said, holding the two handles as she'd done before. "It picks up on magical currents in the ground." She glanced at the butcher and baker, who were focused on the rod and not the surroundings. "But if the soldiers find me using this thing, they'll know I'm up to something, so we need to keep an eye out for them."

"Right," Ida said, turning and watching the road.

"Good so far," Allen replied.

Bev didn't feel the familiar tug until she was right up next to the dark forest. It took her along the tree line, where she was met by the sentient bristles that rustled with warning.

"I'm not going inside again," Bev told the sentient forest. "Unless you're hiding the dam I'm looking for?"

Another rustle that Bev could only assume meant no.

Ida walked beside her, keeping her wary gaze on the road, and Bev followed the sensation of the tugging. The forest bordered the farmlands, and Bev would've been surprised if any of the farmers would willingly give up their precious growing space to be…however the dam was constructed.

"Maybe you're overthinking it," Ida replied, her gaze on the horizon. "Maybe whatever is stopping the river is very small. Disguised to look like a rock. Something inconspicuous."

"I hope not," Bev said. "Because if so, we'll have a devil of a time trying to prove to the townsfolk that the soldiers are causing the earthquakes." She tightened her grip on the dowsing rod, saying a small prayer that they weren't on yet another wild goose chase.

"Hang on." Ida frowned. "Do you hear that?"

"Hear what?" Allen said.

"There's something… I think I hear something squeaking." She turned toward the left. "It's coming from over there."

Bev turned and the dowsing rod tugged in that

direction. "Let's follow it and see where it goes."

"What is…" Bev shook her head. "*That?*"

They'd followed the tugging over hills and through fence lines until they came to an overgrown corner of Alice Estrich's land. There, they'd walked through thick brush until they came across a clearing—and the strangest machine Bev had ever seen in her life.

It was a large…corkscrew, turning and milling in the earth but not getting any deeper. In fact, the corkscrew wasn't actually in the ground, but it was an inch or so above. The machine was dark metal, perhaps iron, and groaned as it churned the sand, sending off spurts of rust—the same orange coating that had been on the soldiers' uniforms.

But the most striking thing wasn't the machine, it was the farmland itself. Behind the machine, where the magic river flowed—perhaps even pooled, Bev didn't know how that worked—the ground was lush, green, almost overgrown with all manner of plants. But beyond, it was dry, dusty, dead. Everything that had grown was withered or brown. It was a stark reminder that Pigsend's vibrant farmlands weren't just thanks to fertile soil and good weather—and the recent crop failures were a direct result of the soldiers' intervention.

"Okay, so that's…it?" Allen asked.

"I haven't the foggiest, but I'd guess yeah." Bev moved to get up when Ida yanked her back down so hard, it would surely leave a bruise. "Hey, what—"

"Shh," Ida said, pointing to the bushes.

Not a moment later, one of the five soldiers walked out, inspected the corkscrew and scribbled something in a small notebook. He closed the book and tucked it in his pants then pulled out a dowsing rod almost identical to the one Bev had, except much more well-worn. He held it between his hands and walked around, perhaps testing to make sure the machine was still stopping the magic, then put it back in his pants.

Without a word, he turned around and left.

The trio waited a few breaths before anyone spoke. "Well, I think that's pretty damning evidence, if I do say so myself," Ida whispered.

"What should we do?" Allen asked.

"Ida, do you think you could carry that thing?" Bev asked.

"Probably," she said. "But should we just rip it out of the ground, or should we turn it off first or what?"

"Your guess is as good as mine," Bev said.

"Wait a minute," Allen said, grabbing both their arms. "What if turning this thing off sends like…a tidal wave of magic into town and causes even more problems?"

Bev looked at Ida, having no experience with magic or magical rivers. Ida opened and closed her mouth then shrugged helplessly.

"Merv doesn't have time for us to worry about that," Bev said. "And besides, not doing anything would probably be worse. Allen, keep watch. Ida, come with me."

Bev emerged from their hiding spot and slowly approached the whirling machine. Bev hadn't a clue how it was operational—it didn't look to be powered by steam or anything else. But there was something about it that tingled her fingertips, like a long-lost memory begging to break the surface. She shook herself and circled the machine, looking for a way to turn it off.

"What do you think, Ida?" she asked.

"Gotta be powered by magic," Ida said, reaching to touch the iron. She winced as she retracted her hand. "Cheese and crackers, that smarts."

"Iron," Bev said. "It's a natural anti-magic material."

Ida glanced at her from around the machine. "And how, pray tell, do you know that?"

"No idea," Bev said with a smile.

"How is it powered by magic if it's an anti-magic material?" Ida asked, rubbing her chin. "That doesn't make sense."

"Well, we don't really need to know how it

works," Bev said with a shrug. "We just need to get it out of the ground, right?" She sighed, glancing at Ida. "But considering I was going to have you lug this thing into town, that does complicate things."

"How so?"

The question was posed so very innocently that Bev almost believed Ida didn't know about her own powers. They were alone out here, no eavesdroppers, but it still felt like a bridge too far for Bev to ask her dear friend what kind of magic she held.

"You said it hurt to touch, right?" Bev said, after a moment's thought. "So it's going to have to be Allen and me."

Ida touched it again and winced. "It's not awful. Just feels like a pinch on my finger."

"Allen," Bev said, turning around. "We need you."

The young baker came running over. "What's up?"

"We've got to pull this out," Bev said, holding onto a handle on the side of the machine. "Take a handle and pull."

Together, they yanked and pulled, but the machine didn't budge an inch. Something had secured it firmly to the ground, and it wasn't going to move through brute force alone.

"Let me help," Ida said, gently pushing Allen out of the way. She winced as she closed her hand around the machine but held on. "Okay, ready?"

She and Bev pulled, but as Bev had suspected, the iron sapped her supernatural strength, and the machine didn't move.

Ida released her grip, a light sheen of sweat on her face as she wiped her forehead. "This thing is nuts," she replied. "I've never… Never in my life…"

"Why don't you keep watch?" Bev said, hoping to avoid the conversation all together. "Allen and I will keep trying."

They did, indeed, try everything. Digging around the base, where the stand was buried into the rich soil, but even when the entire contraption was exposed, there didn't seem to be a way to move it.

"I have a thought," Ida said, walking back over to them. "You said this thing is made of iron, which should stop magic, right?"

Bev nodded.

"What if it's not necessarily stopping the flow of magic, but redirecting it?" Ida asked, kneeling down next to the corkscrew. "What if it's taking the thread of magic and spinning it back that way? And the force of the magic flowing through the screw is what's keeping it in place?"

"I don't see how that's helpful," Allen said, wiping his forehead, but Bev nodded slowly.

"The soldiers called it a diverter," she said.

"And theoretically," Ida said, inspecting the machine from top to bottom closely, "one wouldn't just leave a contraption like this here forever, right? There'd have to be some kind of way to stop the machine so it could be moved, right?"

Bev nodded. "But do you think they'd leave whatever stops it on the machine?"

Ida craned her neck, too short to see over the top of the machine. "Allen, give me a boost, will you?"

The baker knelt, and Ida climbed up on his thigh, now able to see over the top. She reached for something invisible on the top of the machine and winced as she tried to pull it off. "I can't. Bev?"

They switched places, and Bev climbed up onto Allen's knees. Atop the contraption, there was a small bar that seemed fitted into the top, but easily removed by sliding it out (assuming one didn't have magic in their veins). With the small, iron bar in hand, Bev climbed off Allen's knees and stared at it in her hand.

"So if we stick this into the ground a bit farther back in the river—"

"It should stop the flow of magic so we can remove the dam," Ida finished, smiling brightly. "Or so I think. I don't know how any of this works."

"That sounds reasonable enough to me," Allen replied. "Bev?"

"Let's give it a shot." She glanced at the sun. "We don't have much time left."

She walked about ten paces into the lush part of the farmland then drove the iron bar into the ground. Almost immediately, the grass and flowers beyond began to whither and wilt. And just like Ida had predicted, the machine stopped spinning—and fell over.

"Remind me to bring you with me next time I have to do one of these investigations, Ida," Bev said, wiping her brow.

Ida just blushed.

The contraption was now moveable, but it was still heavy as all get-out. Only Bev and Allen could touch it, although Ida did try a few times before both of them barked at her to keep her distance. Bev prayed Allen would keep any suspicions about Ida's strength to himself; then again, his own mother held magic that he'd kept a secret, so perhaps she was safe with him.

"We need a wagon or something," Ida said. "Let me run ahead and find one—"

"It'll take too long," Bev grunted, as she adjusted the heavy machine on her shoulders. "Just need to keep walking."

"Maybe I can try again—" Ida began, but both Bev and Allen shouted, "*No.*"

"We got it," Allen said.

Bev just nodded. Ida had tried to take it from them but dropped it within five seconds.

"I just don't understand what's going on," Ida said, looking at her hands. "I've never had trouble carrying anything before. Never in my life!"

"Are you..." Allen grunted as he shifted. "Are you serious? You don't get what's going on?"

Ida turned to look at them, genuinely confused.

"Your strength is magic," Allen said. "I thought that was pretty obvious."

"Don't be ridiculous," Ida said with a laugh. "I don't have magic."

Bev shook her head. "You do, Ida. It's why you can't carry this ridiculous thing. It's reacting with your magical strength."

"B-but...that's impossible. How could I have magic all this time and not know it?"

"How could you lug around large cow carcasses by yourself without noticing?" Allen grunted.

"Well, I've just always been strong. My parents never mentioned anything about it."

"And why would they?" Bev said. "With all the queen's laws about magic."

"But that's just it. Those laws came into effect five years ago. Surely, someone would've mentioned it sooner," Ida replied. "I suppose they might've thought I was special."

"They didn't have strength like this?" Bev asked.

She shook her head. "They were normal. Perhaps it skips a generation."

"Or twenty," Allen said. "Bev, I might need a break. This thing is killing my back."

"Almost there," Bev said, spying Pigsend in the distance. "Just keep one foot in front of the other."

Up ahead, someone was running toward the trio. Bev squinted, looking for a queen's uniform, but exhaled when she saw it was Vellora. The other butcher waved her arms as if to get their attention as she ran up.

"We aren't walking any faster," Allen grunted.

"Maybe she can help us," Bev said. "I think her strength is natural."

Vellora huffed and puffed as she came up to them, putting her hands on her knees as she caught her breath. "I'm…glad…I…found you."

"What's going on?" Ida asked.

"Rosie summoned…soldiers to…town hall. Will be arresting Merv…if town…finds him guilty."

"I'm sure they're still deliberating, right?" Ida asked.

"No," Vellora said. "They're voting now." She finally noticed the large machine that sat between Bev and Allen. "What in the world is that thing?"

"Hopefully, proof of Merv's innocence," Bev said.

"Do you think this will be enough?" Ida said.

"I don't know," Bev said. "But it's all we've got, so we need to get there before it's too late."

CHAPTER TWENTY~TWO

Even with Vellora's help, the iron corkscrew was still unwieldy. Ida trailed behind, wringing her hands but saying nothing. More than once, Bev considered telling her to leave, to let the three of them bring the machine to the town and deal with the consequences. Would the soldiers arrest her for interfering before they even had a chance to tell the town about it? Would the townsfolk turn against her, as they seemed to have done already? And most importantly, had she dragged three innocent people into her schemes whose lives were about to be upended as well?

But the others wore looks of stoic

determination, marching toward the town without a second thought—at least none Bev could see. And if they believed in her, believed that she was right, then she had to hope the town would, too.

"Almost there." Vellora grunted. "How the heck did they drag this thing around anyway?"

"Horses, probably," Bev replied. "There are five of them at the stables."

"And why didn't we do that?"

"We're almost there," Bev said, as they passed by the inn and bakery. "Almost there."

The final few blocks seemed the longest yet, and Bev had taken some *long* walks in the past few weeks. But as they drew closer to the town hall, the sounds of voting reached Bev's ears.

"…guilty…"

A round of applause followed.

"And Mr. Sterling?" Hendry's voice echoed behind the clapping. "What say you?"

"Guilty."

"We need to hurry," Ida said. "They're almost through the alphabet."

"We're walking as fast as we can," Allen replied, his face covered in sweat. "How do we want to do this? Just barge in with this thing?"

"That was my plan," Bev replied.

The front doors were still wide open, so the three of them awkwardly walked through. The crowd was on their feet, humming with anticipation as they waited for the final votes to be cast and tallied. But as Bev, Vellora, and Allen passed with the large corkscrew, the humming turned to confused conversation.

"What in the..." Earl was near the door. "Whatcha got there, Bev?"

"Answers," she replied.

They continued up toward the front, where Hendry was staring intently at the roll of townsfolk as she counted them off. Rustin was next to her, his head lolling to the side as he snoozed. The five soldiers were nowhere to be seen, so they must not have arrived yet. Merv was seated on the opposite side, his paws resting on his round belly, and he sat up when he saw the three of them. It was hard to tell his expression with his knitted eye mask, but Bev had to assume he could smell the iron from that far away.

"And Ms. Kelooke?" Hendry called, staring at the paper in front of her. "What say you?"

"I say... What the heck is that, Bev?"

Hendry jumped and finally looked up, her brows rising as she took in the sight of Bev, Vellora, and Allen carrying a large metal machine. She opened and closed her mouth a few times, seemingly at a loss for words as she elbowed Rustin. He snorted as he awoke, sitting up straight and wiping his mouth.

"Wh-what's going on? Did we finish?"

"I think we might have a bit of a complication," Hendry said, with a half-smile as the trio finally reached the front of the hall.

With a grunt, they dumped the corkscrew onto the ground, the *boom* echoing in the halls. Bev winced as she glanced at the wooden floor below, hoping they hadn't left a scratch.

"Oh, I need some willow after that," Vellora said, rubbing her neck.

"That'll be all," Bev said. "I'll take it from here."

"You sure?" Allen asked.

"Very." Bev adjusted her tunic as she faced Hendry. "Thanks for your help."

"Bev," Mayor Hendry began, though she didn't look surprised to see them, "we're in the middle of our final votes on Merv's guilt. I hope whatever… you've brought is important and pertinent to that effort."

Bev nodded. "It is. I would like to present new evidence."

"Is there anyone who needs to be present to hear said evidence?" Hendry asked, almost leading Bev to the answer. "I've told the soldiers to come back once we've finished our deliberations."

"They should probably bc here, yes," Bev said.

"Very well." She elbowed Rustin again. "Go find

them."

He rose and left, and Bev stood in front of the large machine by herself in front of the whole town. She couldn't help but feel a little bit nervous. A lot nervous, in fact. She was certainly in over her head, and if this went poorly, then she'd certainly be in some hot water.

The crowd was muttering behind her, and it didn't sound very friendly. Merv had fallen asleep in the corner, his head tilted back and his mouth open as he snored lightly. Hendry had an unreadable expression as she sat in her chair with her hands folded together.

Finally, Rustin returned with the five soldiers in tow. Karolina hadn't taken three steps inside the room before she saw Bev and the machine, and recognition, shock, and anger rolled over her face in quick succession. The other soldiers glanced at each other—almost nervously?—as they followed.

"What in the…" Karolina balled her fists as she walked up the center aisle. "What are you doing with that?"

"Well, we—I—think it's the cause of all the earthquakes," Bev said. "Therefore, I'd like to present new evidence in the trial of Merv the mole. Definitive proof that the real culprits behind the earthquakes are…" she swallowed and leveled her gaze at Karolina, "the queen's soldiers."

A roar of surprise, anger, and disbelief came from the crowd, and Karolina's face twisted into a snarl as she spun to the soldiers behind her.

"Arrest her," she said, pointing at Bev. "For interfering with official royal business."

"Now hold on a second," Hendry said, standing. "I understand you have the jurisdiction to arrest anyone in the country, but we have laws here in Pigsend that must be followed. We are in the middle of a trial—and Bev has come presenting new evidence." She squared her shoulders as Karolina began to heave angry breaths. "The town will hear the evidence, and a new vote will take place."

"Are you *serious*? You just went through two hours of voting." The soldier rolled her eyes.

"That's the law here in Pigsend. And I know the queen's soldiers are keenly interested in following the law, are they not?"

"Hear, hear!" came a call from the crowd.

"Let Bev speak!"

"I want to know what this is!"

More voices added to the chorus, and the brilliance of Hendry's advice to do this in front of a crowd with real evidence became clear. There were at least a hundred-fifty faces staring at the soldiers, some already convinced of their guilt, others incredulous that the queen's soldiers could do such a thing. But if they were to flout the law, everyone in the crowd would've revolted immediately.

"*Fine*," Karolina seethed. "Let her present her *evidence*."

"Very good." Hendry walked back to the table and sat down. "Bev, you have the floor."

Bev hadn't quite rehearsed what she was going to say, but for the first time, she felt it was right and true to tell the whole story—well, the parts that wouldn't get innocent folks in Pigsend in trouble. She started with the gnomes, and how they'd told her that the river had been disturbed, but when she'd returned to them once it was full again, they'd skipped town. Then she described running into Merv, earning a wide, whiskery smile from him as she spoke of his hospitality and the delicious tea—and how he'd told her the gnomes were perhaps referring to a magical river.

At the word *magic*, a gasp of surprise rose from the crowd, and Hendry held up her hands. "Let her finish."

"You know, even looking into unapproved sources of magic is grounds for arrest," Karolina said, glaring daggers at Bev.

"So is, I assume, causing town-shattering earthquakes," Hendry replied lightly, examining her perfectly shaped nails. "Bev, please continue."

The soldier huffed and sat back in her chair, scowling.

"I managed to find the river," Bev said, leaving out the details of how. "And…"

She glanced at Allen, who'd started to look nervous. Talking about his involvement, the barus, and how the soldiers were really looking for a magical object would open an entirely new can of worms. She chewed her lip and decided to skip ahead.

"And so…I stumbled upon this device near the dark forest," Bev said, finally. "I think it's designed to redirect the flow of magic to keep it out of the town." She gestured toward the crowd. "You could see the difference in the crop growth from where the magic river was flowing and where it had been stopped. I'm sure that many of you will find your crops have new life now that we've removed it."

The farmers in the group murmured to themselves, nodding at Bev and glaring at the soldiers, who were starting to squirm behind Karolina. The lead soldier hadn't lost her murderous gaze toward Bev.

"There might be more around town, too. I can't be sure," Bev finished.

"Why were they doing this?" Hendry asked. "Your best guess."

"I don't…quite know," Bev said, although she did know. She didn't want to tell Karolina she'd read her diary or had been eavesdropping in their rooms. "I was hoping they might tell us."

Hendry nodded. "Very well. Thank you for your testimony, Bev." She twisted in her seat to look at the soldiers. "Well? Do you have anything to say in your defense?"

Karolina rose slowly and walked to the center, snorting in Bev's direction threateningly before turning to the crowd. "I am a member of the queen's special service," she replied. "What we do is for Her Majesty. And will not be questioned."

A roar of protest came from the crowd, so loud that it set Karolina back a step or two.

"You must answer for your crimes!"

"My sister nearly died!"

"My beautiful statue was destroyed!"

Hendry let the chorus continue for a few minutes, perhaps for effect, before she raised her hands to quiet the crowd. It took a minute or two for whatever magic the mayor possessed to work its way through the crowd, but finally, there was silence again.

"You might want to try that again, Ms. Hunter," Hendry said, lightly.

Karolina crossed her arms and shook her head. "I don't have to answer to the likes of you."

"I think you'll find that you do," Hendry replied. "Unless you'd like to try your luck against the townsfolk of Pigsend."

"They wouldn't *dare.*"

The crowd groaned again, several farmers coming to their feet. Those who sat in the front talked amongst themselves, glaring at the soldiers. The air in the room was starting to get dangerous, crackling with the anger of a hundred-fifty furious townsfolk.

"You know, we're really far from any other member in the queen's service," Hendry replied sweetly. "If they were to come through town, we could very easily tell them you and your compatriots had simply left and continued on your way."

Instead of telling them of your gruesome deaths was left unsaid but very clearly understood.

"I suggest you speak the truth and do so quickly," Hendry said. "They seem to be losing their patience. And there's only so much I can do to control them."

It was the closest the mayor had ever come to admitting her own special powers, but perhaps the soldier didn't recognize the threat. Bev held her breath as Karolina twisted and snarled and dug in her heels. But she finally seemed to realize the futility of her stance, and her shoulders loosened.

"Fine. It *was* us."

Again, an explosion of anger came from the crowd, and several climbed out of their seats headed toward the soldiers before Hendry, again, held up her hands. Whatever magic the mayor had was in full effect, because they stopped before they could get to the soldier.

"As I said, we have laws in this town, and they *will* be followed," Hendry said. "Now, Ms. Hunter, can you explain to the folks of Pigsend why you stopped the river of magic and destroyed at least two houses?"

Karolina turned, and for the first time, sent a pleading look toward the mayor. But Hendry was stony-faced, and the soldier would get no quarter from her.

"We're on the hunt for a powerful magical object," Karolina said through gritted teeth.

Bev exhaled slightly—so it wasn't anyone in town specifically. For that, at least, she was grateful.

"Our magical finders led us to this town," Karolina continued. "In order to search, we needed all other magic out of the way. And so..." She gestured toward the crowd.

"And so?" Hendry pressed.

"And *so* we installed this magical diversion device," Karolina replied through gritted teeth. "Removing the magic from the town."

"Did you know such a device would cause earthquakes?" Hendry asked.

Karolina licked her lips and shook her head.

But Bev couldn't let her withhold the truth like

that. "That's a lie," Bev replied. "There was another town on the coast that fell into the sea because of their actions."

"*How* did you know about that?" Karolina seethed, glaring daggers at Bev.

"I have my ways," Bev replied with a smirk. "Twiddleston, wasn't it?"

"I heard about that," Hendry said, though Bev was sure that she'd *heard* it from Bev herself. "Nasty business, that. And yet you continued into Pigsend, putting our town in danger."

"It was *important* to the queen that we find this object."

"And did you find it?"

Karolina clicked her tongue. "No."

"Well, as it stands, we can't let you continue to stop the magical river. There's been too much damage to our town."

"Hear, hear!" The crowd had been oddly silent during the exchange, but Etheldra Daws banged her cane against the ground.

"The citizens of Pigsend will pick up the search in your stead," Hendry said, almost a little too brightly. "I'm sure between the lot of us, we can pull together to locate whatever sort of thing you're missing—and we'll be sure to write when we find it."

"What do you mean write—?"

"Citizens of Pigsend," Hendry said, walking from the table to the center of the room, "if you are satisfied with the evidence provided, please say *aye*."

The entire room came back in one voice, "*Aye.*"

"Anyone who wishes to hear more, please say *nay.*"

Not a voice was heard.

"Well, then, sounds like we have our verdict," Hendry said.

"But you just went through two hours of voting, person by person, for the moleman—" Karolina squeaked, gesturing at Merv.

"Oh, right." Hendry turned to Merv with a smile on her face. "Mr. Merv, we are terribly sorry for the miscommunication. Please accept Pigsend's sincere apology and know that you are welcome to come back any time to visit. Our Harvest Festival will be kicking off in the next couple of weeks, and we'd welcome you as an honored guest to join in the festivities."

Merv rose from his haunches and bristled. "That certainly doesn't sound like my type of fun. But I wouldn't say no to having Bev come for another cuppa." He nodded toward Bev. "You know where to find me, Bev."

Bev nodded. "As soon as the inn is repaired, I'll pay you a visit."

"Speaking of," Merv said, as he waddled toward

the door, "I do hope the soldiers who caused all the damage will be offering reparations. Seems a bit unfair for the citizens of Pigsend to front the bill to repair everything."

"Hear, hear!" Stella Brewer said.

"Yes, that's a good point," Hendry said, turning to Karolina. "We will need compensation for the damage caused. I'd say it's a hundred gold for the Brewers' house and maybe fifty for the Weary Dragon Inn—what say you, Earl?"

"Sounds about right," he said, crossing his arms. "Plus a little extra, for our trouble."

Karolina's face was bright red with anger and shock. "This town is going to *hear* it from Her Majesty. Don't be surprised if I come back with fifty soldiers and raze this place to the ground."

"We look forward to it," Hendry said. "Now if you'll be so kind as to leave our town, I think we've had quite enough excitement for one year."

CHAPTER TWENTY~THREE

Bev didn't actually believe they'd leave, but once she finally extracted herself from the congratulatory well-wishes for cracking the case, the inn was deserted, the horses gone. After cleaning the stalls, she walked Sin back to her usual stall and gave her an extra helping of hay and oats, hoping now that the river was flowing again, perhaps she might find some more carrots. The mule ate happily, and Bev patted her on the nose and smiled.

All was right in the world.

With the soldiers gone, the town immediately set to work rebuilding what had been destroyed.

Earl called in a few friends from Sheepsberg, and together they shored up the hole in front of the Weary Dragon Inn and got the wall rebuilt in three days. To repay the favor, Bev spent a few days helping to carry dirt, bricks, and whatever else Earl and his friends needed as they took on the much more difficult task of rebuilding the Brewers' house. The twins took a bedroom at the Weary Dragon Inn, grateful to have a bit more space after spending the past week with Vicky.

Bev finally removed the *Closed for Dinner* sign on the door, eager to find some sort of normalcy once more. But of course, there was one more task to complete before she could put the sinkhole mess to bed for good.

"Mm. Is that rosemary I smell?" Stella said, walking into the kitchen. "Oh, Bev, are you making your bread? Finally?"

Bev smiled as she kneaded the dough, pulling and pushing it across her wooden table. This was the third round she'd made today, with three cooling on the table and another three baking in the oven.

"Figured it was time, you know?" She wiped her forehead with the back of her hand. "Got a lot of folks eager to get a loaf after the help they gave me."

"I think it's us who should be baking for you." Stella was inching closer to the counter loaves, which hadn't quite cooled enough.

"If you're hungry," Bev said, "Allen dropped off some muffins this morning."

Stella turned, her eyes lighting up as she found the basket on the table. Allen was still struggling to make ends meet, but he'd been dropping off half a dozen muffins every morning to Bev to work through his debt to her. Based on the numbers of folks she'd seen in his shop the day before, she had hope he was on his way to getting his business back on track.

"I think they're sweet potato this morning," Bev said.

Stella picked one up and took a bite, and her eyes lit up with joy and pleasure. "Oh, Bev. What did he put in these? It's so moist and..." She shoved the rest of the muffin in her mouth as she moaned happily.

Bev had to smile. These muffins didn't have a lick of pobyd magic in them. It seemed Allen was content to put the magic bauble by his bedside table and *not* use it, rather basking in the glow of his beloved mother's magic. And as Bev had predicted, his baked goods were once again flying off the shelf. Perhaps the pobyd magic wasn't the secret ingredient to Fernley's muffins. Perhaps it was just...love.

Bev chuckled to herself as she sprinkled rosemary into the dough and kneaded it in. The secret ingredient to her bread was most assuredly *not* love, but the rosemary she'd hung to dry three days ago that was finally ready to go into the bread. The earthy fragrance wafted up to her nose and she took a long breath of it.

Not a few seconds later, Shasta walked into the kitchen, licking her lips. "Did I hear Allen dropped off some muffins?"

Stella handed one to her twin and together they shared an unspoken conversation of joy. Shasta shook her head as she swallowed a big bite.

"You know, I should see if Etheldra wants to buy sweets for the tea shop from Allen again," Shasta said. "It's been so long since we've gotten anything this good from him. She has a friend in Sheepsberg who owns a shop there who might want to get stuff from him, too."

"I'm sure Allen would be appreciative," Bev said.

The twins nodded their goodbyes as they headed off to their respective jobs for the day, and Bev finished kneading the dough in the silence of the kitchen. Her nose—and the time on the clock—said that the ones in the oven were finished, so she put the worked dough in a bowl, covered it with a kitchen towel, and stuck it in her usual warming spot close to the oven, but not so close that it would overproof.

She grabbed her well-worn kitchen towels and

pulled the loaf pans from the oven, placing them on the table. The crust was golden brown, and the ends folded over the loaf pans in a perfectly symmetrical shape. But most important was the *smell*, the earthy rosemary smell that filled her with such joy it was hard to stop smiling.

These loaves would take at least an hour or two to cool before Bev could do anything with them, so she left them where they were and focused on the other three that had been sitting there for a while. She dumped them out onto the table, inspecting them for imperfections.

Whatever Stella might think, Bev was eager to repay the favors she'd incurred during the investigation. She didn't like the thought of being in anyone's debt, especially because one never knew when another curiosity might appear in town. She wrapped the loaves in kitchen towels, resting them inside her wicker basket. Then she put aside her apron, made sure to note the time on the clock so she could be back in time to pull the bread from the oven, and headed out into the beautiful day.

After weeks of taunting, fall had finally arrived with cooler temperatures and the smell of crispness in the air. And it hadn't come a moment too soon—the Harvest Festival would be kicking off in a few short weeks, and there was still much to do. Bev had a long list of tasks and cleaning to accomplish, especially after the dusty work of rebuilding the front wall. But that was for tomorrow. Today was for gratitude.

Her first stop was the library, delivering a steamy, lush rosemary loaf to Max, who's eyes lit up when Bev walked in the door.

"Bev, you rascal!" he cried, clapping his hands. "I know you didn't bake me one of those loaves."

"And why wouldn't I?" Bev said, pulling one out and handing it to him. "Thank you so much for your help."

"Don't mention it. That's what I'm here for." But the old librarian was eyeing the loaf with a greedy eye, and Bev had a feeling he'd be hightailing it upstairs to find a knife and a pad of butter as soon as Bev left him.

Her next stop was a bit less…enthusiastic about the bread. Rosie Kelooke sat on her porch, watching Bev approach with a sneer on her face. Her chickens clucked menacingly in the front yard, daring Bev to open the gate.

"I expected this a week ago," Rosie said, rocking back and forth. "I hope you aren't giving me a stale loaf."

"Took it out of the oven earlier this morning," Bev said.

"So cold, then."

Bev chuckled. "Rosie, you know you have to let

them sit to finish cooking, right? I promise, it's going to be fresh and warm as soon as you come get it." She lifted the loaf in the air. "Unless you'd rather I give it to someone else?"

The old woman rose and marched down the stairs. Her chickens made way for her on the path, as if sensing they'd be kicked if they didn't. Bev held her kind smile as Rosie came closer, and the two stared at each other for a long time.

"Here. Thank you for—"

Rosie snatched the bread out of Bev's hand. She brought the loaf to her nose and inhaled, and some of the anger melted from her face.

"This will be fine."

And with that, she turned and walked back to her house, slamming the door.

Bev adjusted the wicker basket on her arm and shook her head. Might be worth getting her *own* willow tree planted in the back of the inn, just to avoid having to deal with Rosie anymore.

~

The destination for Bev's final loaf was a bit farther out of town, but every bit as necessary as the other two. She walked through the verdant hills, smiling as the heliotrope and pink grass swayed in the wind. If she knew where the gnomes had gone, she might have brought them a loaf, too. But her best guess was that they were as far away as the soldiers—and she wasn't about to leave her beloved Pigsend.

With care, she eased herself down the large hole, making sure to keep the loaf of bread covered so it wouldn't get dirty. This part of the tunnel was dark, but she kept walking with her hand pressed to the wall until she reached what appeared to be a fork. She hadn't noticed it when she'd been here the first time with Merv. It was, perhaps, the underground road that connected Merv with the city somewhere beyond. But Merv's door was visible down to the left, so Bev adjusted the basket on her arm and headed in that direction.

She rapped on the large door, stepping back and waiting. There was a bit of commotion on the other side, and the knob turned over as the door opened.

"Oh!" Merv opened the door completely. "Bev. What a lovely surprise. What can I do for you?" He chuckled. "Don't tell me there's another problem you need help with."

"Not today," Bev said, lifting the basket. "I come with a thank-you gift for all your help—and as an apology for all the nonsense of the town meeting last week."

"Oh." He bristled and welcomed her inside. "Bygones, you know. I'm just glad it was all resolved satisfactorily." His whiskers twitched. "My, my, is that rosemary I smell?"

"My famous bread," Bev said, pulling the loaf out and handing it to him. "Baked just for you."

He took the loaf in his claws and turned it over. In the large animal's hands, it was miniscule. "Bit small. But it'll do."

"Next time, I'll have to bake yours in a bigger pan," Bev said.

"Let's have a slice and a cuppa," Merv said, heading toward the kitchen.

"I think I'll have to take a raincheck on that," Bev said, glancing at the clock on Merv's wall. "Got another batch in the oven, and they'll be due to come out soon."

"Oh." Merv's whiskers drooped. "That's a shame."

"How about this—I'll come back in two weeks, after the Harvest Festival," Bev said. "Or you're welcome to come to the inn and spend a night or two. Maybe even submit something to the fiber arts contest?"

He tutted, his whiskers twitching. "I'll certainly have to consider it."

"Excellent."

"And in the meantime, I have some blankets I can send with you."

~

Laden with five new blankets in various colors, Bev made her way back to Pigsend with a whistle and a smile. After pulling the bread from the oven, she wrapped two from the cooling batch in another set of kitchen towels, along with one of Merv's blankets, and headed across the street to the butchers.

"Is that…?" Ida gasped as Bev walked in the door.

"Rosemary bread," Bev announced happily.

"Oh, forget that—is that one of Merv's blankets?" Ida said, taking the blanket from Bev and pressing it to her cheeks. "Goodness me. Is this ours to keep?"

Bev nodded and placed the two loaves on the counter. "For all your help. There's not enough bread in the world to express my gratitude."

"Oh, pshaw," Vellora said, already holding a clean knife as she attacked the bread. "But you know," she popped the heel into her mouth and sighed, "f'is ish a goo' way to say f'ank ew."

"I don't know." Ida cuddled the blanket. "I might have to go pay Merv a visit myself and raid his closet. You can still get to his house? I guess he's not worried about the denizens of Pigsend coming with pitchforks."

"I doubt they'd need to anymore," Bev said. "Unless we get more earthquakes."

"And if we do, we know exactly who to blame," Vellora said with a nasty smile. "Shame I didn't get a chance to knock those soldiers around a bit."

"Yes, what a shame," Ida said, swatting her wife on the arm before kissing her lightly on the cheek. "Glad you're back to your normal cheerful self, love."

"Me, too," Vellora said, beaming at her wife before turning to Bev. "So what's next for you, Bev?"

"Long list of cleaning to tend to," Bev said with a sigh. "Want the place spic and span before the Harvest Festival gets going." She paused. "And, of course, making dinner tonight. What do you have ready for me that goes well with rosemary bread? I have a feeling it's going to be a packed house once word gets out that I've got some ready."

"Oh? Are you back open for dinner?" Ida asked.

Bev smiled. "Everything is back to normal, it seems."

~

Bev walked back across the street, noting the different colors of the ground where the sinkhole had been. She was still a bit leery of walking through the center of it, but soon that would fade. The entire inn had been painted a fresh white, contrasting with the reinforced thatched roof. The sign, too, had been repainted, courtesy of Ida, who'd colored the letters green to match the roof and painted a little red dragon on the bottom to give it a bit of excitement. It was different, but…Bev didn't mind it so much. It felt a bit more like *her* place now, and not just that she was taking care of it for ol' Wim.

She walked inside, running her hand along the long table in the center, and idly wondering how many folks would show up for dinner. The bread was already made, but she wanted to add another side dish, in case there was a *big* crowd. She had a full root cellar now, but she just couldn't decide what to make. So she headed out back to her garden for some inspiration.

Sin brayed at her from the stall, and Bev popped in to give her a carrot.

"You're gonna get spoiled, old girl," Bev said with a laugh.

She walked to her garden and put her hands on her hips, gazing out at the collection of rosemary, thyme, oregano, sage…

Something caught her eye to the left of the garden. She frowned as she walked over to the half-buried yellow thing in the ground. Kneeling, she brushed the dirt away from it, pulling out…

"What in the…?"

It was definitely *something*, but what? It was made from some heavy material—not metal, not wood, nor rock, but something in between. There was a clear design in the center, but the edges were jagged, like it had been broken. She glanced around the surrounding area, looking for the other pieces, but...

No, this was the only piece. The rest had been scattered across the continent.

Bev shook herself, the voice coming from somewhere deep inside her. It was so sure of itself, an echo of a life that existed just beyond Bev's recollection.

And she knew, without a shadow of a doubt, that *this* was the powerful object the soldiers had been looking for.

She exhaled loudly, a chill coming over her, even as she sat in the warm sun. She could do as Hendry had said they would, write to the soldiers and let them know the object had been found, but...

But this object had been hidden for a reason. And it was best that it stayed that way.

So Bev turned to her herb garden and dug a deep hole between the thyme and rosemary plants. Then she deposited the amulet in the ground and covered it with dirt. The plants would grow over it, hopefully, and that would be the end of it.

She rose, dusted herself off, and headed back into the kitchen, intent on making dinner and re-forgetting she'd ever seen the amulet.

Bev continues her adventures in

FIENDS AND FESTIVALS

Weary Dragon Inn

BOOK TWO

Acknowlecments

Bev was a complete surprise from start to finish. I have to say, it was the coziest, most relaxing book to write, and I'm so excited to continue with this fun cast of characters that have come into existence.

As always, the biggest thanks goes to my husband, who supports my dreams like no one else—especially through the chaotic mess that was November of 2022 when I drafted this book. Between pregnancy scares, birthdays, Thanksgivings, and saying goodbye to our beloved Biscuit, it was a miracle that I did anything at all. But thanks to you, I managed to keep my head on straight and get it done. Shout-out also goes to my parents, my mother-in-law, and my aunt for taking the toddler so I could work.

My thanks to Natasia and Luke at Stardust Book Services for the brilliant map, Robert Ardy for the brilliant cover, my beta readers Kelsey, Drea, Ybelline, and Elisia, Danielle Fine, my editor, and my typo checkers Heather and Blake.

Thanks also must be paid to the MI(L)F Discord group, without whom I wouldn't have been nearly as productive. A good writing group is essential to a writer's sanity, and sprinting with you guys was so much fun.

KICKSTARTER BACKERS

A heartfelt thank you to the Kickstarter backers who so generously supported the first three books in the series:

Aaron Frost, Aaron Jamieson, Abby Brew, Abigail Conner, Abra Roth, Adam Cole, Adam Kerstin, Adrianne Carley, AingealWroth, Alaska Momster, Alessandro Colombo, Alexandra Fluskey, Allison Torres, Alyssa Emmert, Amanda Gerdel, Amy Chadwick, André Laude, Andrew Kaplan, Andy, Anil Kadam, Ann Cofell, Anna, Anonymous, aoife & ryan, Archibald Nastyface Hethrenton, Aruhi, Ashley Matics, Ashley Stark, Becca Stillo, Becky B, Becky Carr, Becky James, Bethany Pratt, Bettina Pickett, Blake Strickland, Blumpsie, Boris Veytsman, Bree, Brett Werst, Brian Bauer, Bridget Horn, Bridgette Findley, Brock Miller, C. A. Maxwell, Caitlyn M Nye, Caitlyn Miller, Camilla Vavruch, Carlos Guerra, Carly Occhifinto, Catherine Sampson, CAVE321, Chase Sanders, Chelsea, Chris A McGee, Chris King, Chris Ward, Christa Rumage, Christa S. Rickard, Christian Holt, Christiana Laudie, Christine Crew, Clarissa Gosling, Cody L. Allen, Colin Letch, Conor, Cullen 'Towelman' Gilchrist, Dale A Russell, Danielle Perry, Dave and Rose Fonville, Dave Baughman, Dave Luxton, Dave Marchetti, David Haskins, David Holzborn, David Lewis, Day Leitao, Dead Fishie, DeeAnna, Dexter

Jacobs, Doris Wooding, Douglas & Nicole Williams, Drea Laj, Dustin Thatcher, E. Snelgrove, E.M. Middel, E.V. Everest, E.V. Green, Eddie Joo, Edward E., Elise Roberts, Elizabeth F, Elle Wilson, Ellen Pilcher, Emily Gibbs, Emma Cohan, Emma S, Erica Blumenthal, Erika Jo, Eva Ali, Felicia, Gary Olsen, GhostCat, Gina Lucas, Gina Points, Ginny L., Golinssohn, Grace Parsons, Greg Rice, Greg Tausch, Gretchen, Hana Correa, Hannah, Heather A. McBride, His & Hearse Press, Hollow Mask, Hollysbookadventure, Howard Blakeslee, Isabel Johnson, J R Forst, J Truscott, Jan Birch, Jan Dierker, Janelle Boys-Chen, Jean Sitkei, Jeffrey M. Johnson, Jennifer, Jennifer Brown, Jennifer Eaton, Jennifer Katsch, Jeremy S, Jesi Blair, Jessi Pike, Jessica Guyette, Jessica Stanton, Joe G, Joe Monson, Joel silvey, John Idlor, John Markley, Johnathan Detrick, Jolene Pierce, Jonathan Snavely, Josh Samples, Joshua, Julia Byers, KA Ramadorai, Kanyon Kiernan, Karen Fonville, Karen Low, Karen Scharff, Karen Tankersley, Karley Rech, Kat Brady, Kat James, Kate Ehrenholm, Katie, Katie L. Carroll, Katie VanWyhe, Katrina Drake, Kaycee Castleman, Keelyn Wright, Keli, Kelsey Hunt, Kenneth Brown, Kiera Storch, Kourtney & William Stauffer, Krissy Pallen, Kristen & Eric Terlep, Kristian Handberg, Kristin Paine Wallin, KRR Lockhaven, Krysti Matheson, Kurt Beyerl, Lacey Holloway, Larry Couch, Laura L Nelson, Lauren Kildea, Leslie Twitchell, Lindachelle, Lindsey Ferebee, Lindsey Thurman, Lisa Henson, Liz Jordan, Lorin Jones, Luke Italiano, M. H. Woodscourt, Marc D Long, Marcus U, Marilyn Donahue, Marine Lesne, Mark T. Eckstein, Marte Myrvold, Matthian, MC, Meghan

DiMarco, Melanie Pokroy, Melissa, Melissa C, Michael B Mitchell, Michael J. Sullivan, author, Michał Kabza, Michelle E. LaCrosse, Molly J Stanton, Nathaniel Webb, Nicole wagner, Niels-Peter, Nikita Johnson, None, Noreen Gwilliam, Oliver Gross, OwainB, Patricia Miller, Patrick Moore, Paul, peter jockel, Phil Beneker, pjk, Polina "Polinchka" Bazlova, prefer not to be named :), R.J. Marchetti, Rachel S., Rachel Stoddard, Rafi Spitzer, Ramón Terrell, Raphael Bressel, Ray Lorenz, Raymond B, Rebecca, Rebecca Buchanan, René Schultze, Renee, Richard Deltoro, Richard Novak, Richard Sayer, Risa Scranton, Rob Steinberger, Robert K. Barbour, Robert Sanders, Robert Stuart, Roman Pauer, Rowan Stone, Russell Ventimeglia, Ryan C., Ryan Scott James, Samantha Eckiss, Samantha Landstrom, Sandy Garza, Sarah, Sarah B, Sarah L. Stevenson, Scantrontb, Scott Casey, Scott Walker, Sean Bradley, Sebastian Ernst, Señor Neo, Serena M, Seth Alexander, Shadowfall, Shaelei, Sierra Davenport, Sissel K. H. Rasmussen, sonoghen, Sophia, Stefke Leuhery, Stephanie Bailey, Stephanie Horn, Stephanie Webb, Stephany, Stephen, Stephen Kotowych, Steve Locke, Steve Untch, Susan Buescher, Suzann P, Taylor Winsor, Terri Connor, Terry, Terry Evans, Momma, Tessa, TF Drifter, The Calderon-Medina family, The Creative Fund by BackerKit, The Freeman Family, Theresa Snyder, Tom Dean, Tony, Tracy Popey, V G Murray, Valerie Bolster, William J. Robbins, Wineke Sloos, xellos, Yngve J. K. Hestem, Zero

ALSO BY THE AUTHOR

The Princess Vigilante Series

Brynna has been protecting her kingdom as a masked vigilante until one night, she's captured by the king's guards. Instead of arresting her, the captain tells her that her father and brother have been assassinated and she must hang up her mask and become queen.

The Princess Vigilante series is a four-book young adult epic fantasy series, perfect for fans of Throne of Glass and Graceling.

THE SEOD CROI CHRONICLES

After her father's murder, princess Ayla is set to take the throne — but to succeed, she needs the magical stone her evil stepmother stole. Fortunately, wizard apprentice Cade and knight Ward are both eager to win Ayla's favor.

A Quest of Blood and Stone is the first book in the *Seod Croi* chronicles and is available now in eBook, paperback, and hardcover.

Also By the Author

The Madion War Trilogy

He's a prince, she's a pilot, they're at war. But when they are marooned on a deserted island hundreds of miles from either nation, they must set aside their differences and work together if they want to survive.

The Madion War Trilogy is a fantasy romance available now in eBook, Paperback, and Hardcover.

empath

Lauren Dailey is in break-up hell, but if you ask her she's doing just great. She hears a mysterious voice promising an easy escape from her problems and finds herself in a brand new world where she has the power to feel what others are feeling. Just one problem—there's a dragon in the mountains that happens to eat Empaths. And it might be the source of the mysterious voice tempting her deeper into her own darkness.

Empath is a stand-alone fantasy that is available now in eBook, Paperback, and Hardcover.

About the Author

S. Usher Evans was born and raised in Pensacola, Florida. After a decade of fighting bureaucratic battles as an IT consultant in Washington, DC, she suffered a massive quarter-life-crisis. She found fighting dragons was more fun than writing policy, so she moved back to Pensacola to write books full-time. She currently resides there with her husband and kids, and frequently can be found plotting on the beach.

Visit S. Usher Evans online at:
http://www.susherevans.com/

Made in United States
Orlando, FL
03 November 2024

53440473R00186